FORBIDDEN MANUSCRIPT

FORBIDDEN MANUSCRIPT

LUBOV LEONOVA

Contents

"What if it's us who create a new version of future reality?
We just need to believe in it and act accordingly."

- Lubov Leonova
Excerpt from *Forbidden Manuscript*

Part 1

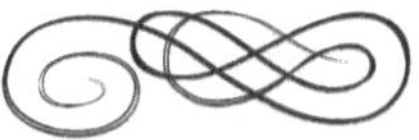

Forgotten Truth

1

Anniversary

The chilly morning wind brushed against the curtains, causing them to flutter against the window. Elisa sat up in bed, rubbing her eyes as she took in the sight of her empty bedroom. The only reminder of the previous night with Jackie was the wrinkled sheets. *Had Jackie already left for work?* Elisa let out a sigh. Regretfully, their busy schedules often kept them apart. Jackie had left without even saying good morning.

Her bare feet touched the cold wooden floor as Elisa made her way to the window to close it. Outside, a new day had dawned, with gentle sun rays illuminating the rooftops and half-naked trees. The deserted street below was coming to life, with shopkeepers in gray coats opening their doors. It was Wednesday, a typical workday for most, but not for the guardians like Elisa. For her, it was one of the quieter days, as the lawbreakers tended to take a break before the busy weekends.

Middle Lake was renowned as a criminal capital, with its history of gangs and illegal activities. It had been three years since the leader of the drug gang was apprehended, but new criminals had since risen to take their place. This turnover in criminal leadership had made Elisa and Jackie's jobs even busier, often causing their days off to not align for weeks at a time. Elisa missed Jackie deeply on days like today, but she never voiced her complaints aloud. After all, she had willingly chosen her duty despite the challenges it presented.

The sound of the entrance door squeaking open caught Elisa's attention, and her heart leaped with joy as she saw Jackie entering the room. Jackie was dressed in a black coat over her work clothes, her hair now dyed a captivating charcoal-black shade that cascaded over her shoulders.

"Where have you been?" Elisa asked, surprised by Jackie's sudden appearance.

"Guess," Jackie replied, placing a paper bag on the floor and beginning to remove her boots. "You're the detective here, after all."

Elisa gave her a puzzled look. "Well, you'll have to give me another hint then."

"Do you know what day it is today?" Jackie asked, her eyes flicking to the calendar on the wall. Elisa's heart quickened as she read the date: *November 2nd*. How could she have forgotten their anniversary? Elisa hadn't even bought a present for Jackie, which was completely unacceptable. But she still had time to come up with something.

"Happy anniversary, my dear," Elisa said, smiling. "I bet you thought I'd forgotten."

Jackie shook her head. "I don't believe you remembered. You look surprised."

Elisa had a ready excuse. "I'm just excited to see your face tonight when I reveal my present."

"Okay, okay," Jackie relented with a laugh. "I know you've been working six days in a row. I'll buy it."

Elisa crossed her arms. "You should trust me more."

Jackie lifted the paper bag, and the scent of warm baking with strawberries wafted through the room. Elisa's stomach rumbled, craving a mouth-watering breakfast.

They sat in their cozy kitchen at a table adorned with a white cloth featuring a forget-me-not pattern. Elisa's aunt had gifted her this cloth as a graduation present when she and Jackie had started living together. Elisa sighed, wishing her aunt knew the true nature of her relationship with Jackie, beyond just being neighbors and best friends. However, she had already caused her aunt enough trouble, and revealing the full extent of their bond might shatter her heart.

Jackie set her coffee cup down on the table. "Ah, Lissy. I've been planning something special for us all this time."

Elisa finished the last bite of pastry and smiled. "This romantic breakfast is the perfect way to start the day. We can continue celebrating in the bedroom."

Jackie's eyes sparkled with mischief. "I can't afford to be late for work. Again."

Elisa reached out and gently wiped the remaining crumbs of pastry from Jackie's chin. "Are you sure?"

"Patience," Jackie replied, brushing her hand away. "Actually, I have a real present for you."

"Darling, you don't need to buy me anything. Your thoughtfulness is more than enough."

She stood up. "Wait here."

Elisa raised her coffee cup. "Alright."

Jackie hurried to the bedroom and rummaged through a drawer, her voice softly humming a tune. Elisa gazed out the window, noticing that the shops were now open. She contemplated buying something beautiful for Jackie, who had a fondness for shiny things. The trade street boasted numerous jewelry stores, and Elisa even had some savings she could dip into for the occasion.

Returning to the kitchen, Jackie held a leather notebook, her cheeks flushed with excitement. "Guess what it is?"

Elisa gave her a puzzled look. "Are you suggesting I start a diary?"

"Nope."

Setting her empty coffee cup down, Elisa remarked, "Good, because I believe diaries only bring trouble."

Jackie sat down and placed the notebook in front of Elisa. She ran her fingers over the cover, which bore the inscription *Our Memoir*.

Looking up at Elisa, Jackie held her breath.

"Is this your story? Have you finished it?" Elisa asked.

She nodded. "*Our* story. I've had so many experiences over the years that didn't quite fit into my diary. So, I started writing about us, about everything that happened since the Academy. And voila, now I have a novel!"

Elisa flipped the first pages, skimming the lines. "I see you've included some personal moments."

"Personal moments, as you call them, make it more interesting," Jackie replied, her eyes sparkling mischievously.

"Who said that?"

"Beth. My literary agent."

Elisa paused before responding. "When did you get an agent?"

"Did you know that Theo spent a significant part of his childhood under the roof of the bookstore? He made some connections in that world."

"Theo is in Triville now, caught up with Rei and investigations. I doubt he had time to assist you with your manuscript."

Jackie waved her hand in explanation. "In case you forgot, we live in a modern world, and we have mail! Theo simply sent the letter to the bookstore owner, who then introduced me to the agent. She's actually a nice woman."

Elisa shook her head in disapproval and closed the book with a thud. "So, you've decided to share our story with the whole world. Why didn't you consult me first?"

Her eyes dimmed. "I thought you would appreciate it. I put in so much effort."

Elisa stood and wrapped her arms around Jackie's shoulders. "I'm sorry. I didn't mean to upset you, especially not today. But you know how challenging it is for us to be who we are, and I just want to protect you."

"Can you at least give it a chance and read it?" Jackie's emerald eyes pleaded. "I can edit out anything you find too revealing."

"Of course," Elisa replied, gently brushing an eyelash off Jackie's cheek. "Please don't take it personally, my love. You know I can be too blunt at times."

Jackie chuckled. "Oh, I know."

"Then go to work, and I'll prepare something special for you tonight. Deal?"

"Deal." Jackie sealed the agreement with a strawberry-scent kiss.

After Jackie left for work, Elisa settled into bed with the notebook titled *Our Memoir*, fully intending to find something incriminating to delay its publication and sway Jackie's decision. However, as she delved into the pages, she found herself increasingly engrossed in their story. Elisa believed she had faced challenges during her time at the Academy, but now, viewing her life from a new perspective, she has discovered more about Jackie and their friends. Despite moments that brought tears to her eyes, she persisted in reading.

As Elisa turned the final page, she noticed the sun hanging low in the sky. Glancing at the bright green time crystal on her nightstand, indicating it was nearly four o'clock, she realized she had spent the entire day in bed.

Elisa rose and began to dress. Despite her reservations about sharing their forbidden love with others, she couldn't deny that Jackie's book was a compelling story that deserved a chance.

Elisa put on her coat and stood still in the middle of the room, faced with yet another dilemma. After uncovering so much about Jackie through the memoir, she was unsure of what gift could match the significance of the book.

Approaching the drawer, Elisa reached for the top shelf and retrieved a jewelry box. Inside, a heart-shaped necklace sparkled, catching the light. She held it in her palm, feeling her heart race with emotion.

Though she may not have believed in its supposed power, the necklace held sentimental value for both of them, symbolizing their connection. Elisa turned the pendant in her hand, noting that it was not broken; only the chain needed replacing. With a smile, she tucked the necklace into her pocket. Now, she had an idea of the perfect gift to complement their shared story.

2

Where the Heart Might Lead

T he jewelry shop was almost empty. Elisa walked along the showcases, which were lit up with glowing yellow and white flowers. Examining the stand with chains, she deliberated if one silver coin was a reasonable price.

"Are you getting a birthday present?" A sales associate smiled at her. She was a woman in her mid-thirties with curly flaming hair and freckles on her pale nose. She wore a long-sleeve white shirt and a dark blue neckerchief, matching her eyes.

"It's more like an anniversary present," Elisa said. "For my … good friend."

"Oh, that's so lovely." The woman pressed her palms together in awe. "What's her name?"

Elisa paused. "How do you know it's her?"

She moved her hand over the showcase. "These are the chains for women. Do you need one for a man?"

Elisa shook her head. "It's for Jackie."

"She is a special one, isn't she?"

"Absolutely." Elisa took the heart-shaped pendant out of her pocket. "Can you help me with that? I want everything to look spotless."

"Of course," the woman said. She pulled out the tray of a display case and took a cassette with the chains. "Let's see what I can do about it."

The entrance door opened, and someone quietly walked in. Elisa glanced back. It was a girl about ten years old, and she looked around with her big blue eyes. She wore a shabby blue coat that obviously didn't protect her from the cold because she was shaking.

Another seller, a young but grumpy-looking man, frowned at her. "Hey, get out of here!"

Elisa gave him a spiteful look. "Come on. She's just a child."

"A child!?" He said with a frank contempt in his voice. "I know these cursed creatures; they are looking to steal something."

Elisa stared at the girl. *Cursed creatures.* This is what Mages called Incapables, people without powers. Incapables weren't rare in this city. They earned this nickname because they usually took low-paid and dirty jobs that were more suitable for them than for educated mages.

Living in Middle Lake, Elisa had gained the same attitude toward them. But now, she couldn't remember why. After all, this girl was just a regular kid who was cold and probably hungry.

"Where are your parents?" Elisa asked softly.

The girl gave her a sad, silent look and walked outside. Forgetting about the jewelry she was supposed to buy, Elisa followed her.

A gust of cold wind hit her in the face as Elisa rushed along the trade street. The naked trees with crooked branches swung under the wind, waving their not-so-happy greetings to the cold weather.

Even the solid houses of gray stones seemed to wither like a bunch of scared chickadees.

"Wait!" Elisa shouted as they neared the crossroad.

The girl stopped. Her blue eyes, like two glaciers, gleamed as she turned. "What do you want?"

Elisa came closer. "I want to help."

She took a step back. "I saw you in the streets. You're a guardian."

"Guardians help people, don't you know that?"

She gave her a sharp look. "Once the guardian rescued me."

"You see –"

"But," she interrupted, "The others didn't like it. Your people found our community and set it on fire. My parents died. I have only a brother, and he told me not to trust the guardians anymore."

Elisa paused. It was hard to find the proper words to make this girl trust 'her people.' "I'm so sorry. Some guardians are not good people, and once I arrested one of them."

She averted her eyes. "I shouldn't talk to you."

Elisa took out her purse and found a silver coin she planned to spend today. She gave it to the girl. "Here. Buy yourself something warm to wear."

She took the coin with her small fingers, covered with mud. "I'm not allowed to take it."

"Let it be our little secret, then."

She nodded and put the money in her pocket.

"What's your name, girl?" Elisa asked.

"Maya."

She smiled. "I'm Elisa."

"Thank you so much, Elisa." Her face became alarmed. "I need to go now. If my brother sees us talking, he will kill me."

"Of course."

Maya smiled and ran away. Her shabby coat disappeared around the corner.

"I can't believe it," a familiar man's voice said behind her back.

Elisa flinched and turned to face the man in a guardian uniform. His shoulder-length hair was brushed into a tail, and his hazel eyes glared at her with uncovered pretension. *Urchin.*

"Are you at work or just walking around, scaring the shit out of people?" She inquired.

He ignored her taunting. "I was trying to establish contact with these kids for months with no success. And you just did it. How do you always do that?"

"Do what?"

"Steal my thunder."

"I didn't mean to –"

"Let me explain what I mean." He put his hands in his pockets. "I bet you are familiar with the situation when you go out of the club and wait for a carriage in a cold street, sometimes for half an hour. Then the sneaky guy appears on your way and steals your carriage from under your nose."

She rolled her eyes. After three years, Urchin still couldn't forgive her for stealing Jackie. Even though they agreed to bury the hatchet as they worked together in the same Guardian House, Urchin was cold with Elisa and really warm with Jackie. Like it could change anything. For years, Elisa tried to find a way to return their friendship, but he was as hard as a rock.

"Incapable kids... Is that the secret project you are working on?" Elisa asked to change the subject.

Urchin hesitated for a moment. "Let's pretend I didn't tell you anything."

"Fine. But still, you could use my help. Just in case you didn't know – I'm good with kids."

He chuckled. "I see. But Lieutenant Walt won't let anyone else into this case."

"Fine. Take your time to think it through. And if you change your mind, you know where to find me." Elisa turned on her heels and walked along the street.

She returned to the doors of the jewelry store and stood motionless, looking at her own puzzled reflection. *Who am I kidding?* She knew she wouldn't be able to buy a gift for Jackie because she had just given money to the girl. But she still had several bronze coins, so at least she could satisfy her hunger and buy something for dinner tonight.

Urchin found her in a cafe as Elisa was finishing her soup. She wiped her lips with a napkin and eyed him curiously. "Did you use a Searching spell to find me?"

He looked down at her. "There was no need to waste my energy. It's the only cheap place to eat close to your home, so I simply came here."

She ignored his mocking. "What do you want?"

He sat on the chair and turned to the dirty window. "I never thought I would tell it to you, but –"

"You need my help," Elisa helped him finish the sentence.

He nodded and went straight to business. "These kids. They appeared in the city this summer, and we think they've organized their own criminal gang."

His words made her drop her spoon. "Incapable kids? Criminals? Are you in your right mind?"

"I know, it sounds odd even for me, but just think about it – no one would suspect a kid, especially an Incapable one. People think Incapables are stupid, but it's stupid to think so. They are like rats, almost invisible and extremely sneaky. And as you know, they don't leave energy traces, so our usual approach doesn't work."

"And what exactly are they doing?"

Urchin lowered his voice. "They steal small things from jewelry stores."

"Like what?"

"Rings, brooches, bracelets. The odd thing – it's all copper stuff, one of the cheapest metals on this market."

Elisa twisted her hairlock, thinking. "That's interesting. What do we know about this metal?"

"I didn't think of it." Urchin shrugged his shoulders. "But we can ask them when we catch them stealing."

"The kids might not know all the details."

"Of course, but they can lead us to their boss. I've been spying on some of the kids for several months, and here is what they have in common – they all communicate with the same Incapable young man named Eric. All I need is to catch him, but he disappeared somewhere."

"I think I can help you," Elisa said.

He nodded. "Then let's meet tomorrow at Lieutenant Walt's office. I'll tell him that you will work with us from now on."

"Good."

The waitress neared the table, and Elisa gave her two bronze coins. Even though Elisa was a loyal customer, she couldn't afford generous tips. The waitress took the money, shook her head, and walked away.

Elisa stood up, and Urchin followed her to the evening street.

It was getting colder outside, and Elisa wrapped herself in her black coat. She looked at her empty purse with regret. "I just tried to be kind to that Incapable girl, and now I'm broke."

"Yeah, it sucks," he said, yawning.

"I went to buy a present for Jackie, and now I don't know what to do."

Urchin's look changed when he heard his ex-girlfriend's name. "You know what, I'll cover the cost."

"Really?"

He nodded. "Of course. Count it as the miscellaneous expenses for this investigation."

"Then I need to visit one store before it's closed."

He took his purse out. "How much?"

3

Guilty by Default

The doors of the meeting room opened with a heavy squeak. Jackie suppressed an urge to smirk with disgust. It had been a while since the remand center became her permanent workplace. However, she still couldn't get used to these dull gray stone walls and horrifying doors.

Jackie sat motionless at her desk as the guard let the new suspect in. This time, it was a young woman with bruises on her neck and shoulders and empty dark brown eyes. She wore a bright orange robe, marking her as a person who had stepped on the dark side of the law. Jackie gave her a compassionate look.

"Carry Wilson?" Jackie asked.

She nodded in silence.

"I'm your lawyer, Jacqueline Robinson, but you can call me Jackie."

Her swollen lower lip trembled. "Am I allowed to have a lawyer? After everything I did?"

"Yes. Don't worry. We'll just talk a bit." Jackie waved her hand, inviting Carry to have a seat.

Carry sat in her chair and lowered her eyes.

Jackie placed a case folder in front of her and opened it. A picture of a woman in a hospital bed was among the handwritten reports and a couple of doctor's notes. She was unconscious, with her heavy eyelids closed shut, and it was hard to recognize her. Jackie pointed at the picture. "Is it you?"

Carry nodded.

"What happened that day? Please tell me as much as you can remember."

"It was my fault." Her voice became quiet. "I left the chicken in the oven that day and went to finish the laundry. When I came back..." A tear slid down her cheek, and she wiped it using the back of her palm. "Everything was in smoke. I remember I started screaming, and the neighbors ran out. They helped me to kill the fire."

Jackie's heart skipped a beat. "Did you get hurt in this accident?"

"No. But later that day, my husband came after, and ... he got really upset. He just painted the kitchen this summer."

Jackie knitted her eyebrows. "I see. Does he often get 'upset'?"

She shrugged. "No more than usual. But this time, I was upset, too. And to my own shame, I broke the rules of our Divine community – to never fight back. I don't know how it happened. He hit me several times, and I... I couldn't handle it, and I just pushed him away using my Telekinesis Gift. He stumbled and fell on something sharp."

Jackie took a medical report. "That's right. He fell on the sharp piece of wood and lost consciousness. Did you take him to the hospital?"

Carry nodded. "Me and two neighbors. One of them has a carriage."

"You have good neighbors."

"I did have... They helped me without asking anything, but I couldn't bear this guilt. I was so sloppy, and I deserved a punishment. So I walked here, but instead of listening to me, they placed me in a medical department." She pointed at the picture in a folder, her index finger shaking. "In the morning, someone reported my husband's death, and I was finally moved to the remand center. Here, I will accept my punishment."

Jackie let out a heavy sigh. This case wasn't easy. None of them were. Because Carry, like many other young women, wasn't familiar with the definition of self-defense. Moreover, women like her considered it as 'their fault,' 'lack of obedience,' and so on. It had been four years since the new law was accepted in the Lake Kingdom. This law was meant to protect women from the cruelty of men. But even the law was helpless if they considered themselves 'guilty.' The trickiest part was changing their mind.

Jackie put her palms together, focusing on finding the proper words to persuade Carry to sign the papers. Fortunately, she had a trick up her sleeve. "I'm so sorry for everything you went through. Once, I was in a really bad situation myself, and I know how it feels. But blaming yourself won't help you feel better."

"What will help, then?"

Jackie lowered her voice. "Forgiveness."

Carry raised her eyes, her eyelashes covered with tear droplets. "I pray for it every day."

"Maybe you need to attend your late husband's funeral," Jackie suggested. "It always helps."

"Even if I'm allowed to attend his funeral, I'm afraid I can never be forgiven for what I've done."

"You can always try. If you ask for it sincerely, in front of his relatives and Divine, you will see what happens." Jackie took a blank piece of paper and placed it in front of Carry. She must make her sign it before the doubt took over. "Here. You only need to sign the paper promising not to leave the city before the investigation ends. Then you can walk out of the remand center."

Carry skimmed the paper, hesitating. "Where will I stay all this time? I don't really want to disturb my neighbors with my presence."

"Don't worry about it." Jackie gave her a pen. "I'll make sure you will stay in a very special place. We have a shelter for women like you."

Her hand stopped halfway. "Like me?!"

Jackie bit her tongue. *Fast. Too fast.* Why on earth didn't she wait for her to put a signature on the paper? In a shelter, they would have a different conversation. She had seen it many times – surrounded by women who stood against domestic violence, even the most broken women didn't feel so guilty anymore.

"I mean women of your age." Jackie corrected herself. "Please sign at the bottom."

"Alright." Carry signed and put the pen away.

Jackie folded the paper. "I'll just tell you one thing before we part."

"Of course." Carry gave her a trustworthy look.

"You will avoid prison as it was clearly an accident."

"No!" Carry yelped. "He died because of me, so I must accept my punishment!"

Jackie exhaled a heavy sigh. This was the worst part, but she couldn't keep her in the dark anymore. "Well, you've just signed the paper promising to behave well. They have no reason to keep you here any longer, so you will be out in an hour. Our carriage will wait for you outside."

She waved her hands in frustration. "You know what? I think I don't need a lawyer anymore... I refuse your services!"

"Too late for that." Jackie collected the paperwork and hid the case file in her briefcase. "Listen, Carry, you are a young woman and have your whole life ahead of you. In prison, if you admit your guilt, you will wear your power-blocking bracelets for so long that it will damage your magic channels. You must not let this accident ruin your whole life."

Carry stood up. "What a pretentious person you are! You'll never understand what it means – to be pure of soul!" Throwing a despising look, she turned and walked to the door, where the prison guard was waiting for her. With that, she left the room.

Her cup of coffee was waiting for Jackie in the corner of her desk. She didn't have a chance to touch it since the day had started, and now it was cold. She took a sip without tasting it. *What a heavy talk!* Her ears still throbbed from Carry's screams. But it was worth it – from now on, she would be taken care of, and things would improve. At least, Jackie hoped so. She put her coffee cup down and chose another case file from a pile on her desk.

4

A Present

In the evening, Elisa sat in the kitchen, admiring a heart pendant. It now had a real chain, shining in the candlelight with pride. She had acquired this pendant from her good old friend Julia, who told Elisa it would help her find true love if she wore it.

To be honest, Elisa never thought she would fall in love again. She never wore it, hoping to get rid of this thing as soon as possible. She kept it in her jewelry box for months before she gave it to Jackie, and after their first argument, she hid it in the deepest place of her closet. Elisa almost forgot about it; however, love mysteriously found its way back to her heart. Elisa smiled. When she got into the Academy, she didn't dare to think that love was possible for her. Then she feared it, thinking it might ruin their careers. It was a big step for her to let Jackie into her life, and even after they finally got back together, only a few people knew about their relationship. Today marked three years since they had started dating and subsequently moved in together.

The entrance door swung open, and Jackie walked in. Slowly, she removed her coat and hung it on the rack. Elisa discreetly tucked the pendant under a napkin to delay revealing her present.

Jackie entered the kitchen and gazed at Elisa with her slightly blurred green eyes. "Sorry, I'm a bit late."

"It's okay," Elisa replied, stealing a glance at the purple-glowing time crystal above the stove, indicating it was around eight in the evening. It wasn't too late, but with the darkening sky and daily fatigue setting in, it felt later.

Jackie settled into her chair and let out a yawn.

"Someone had a hard day," Elisa teased, attempting to lighten the mood.

"I'm a bit tired. Had twelve meetings today. Three of them with the new 'suspects,'" Jackie explained.

Elisa nodded in understanding. "How many did you manage to assign to the healing program?"

"Just one," Jackie replied, rubbing her forehead. "Unfortunately, most of them choose to sit in prison voluntarily. They are too broken to even consider a life free of violence."

"Well, one out of three is a good result," Elisa offered, giving her an encouraging smile. "I remember how challenging it was in the beginning."

"It was. That's why I'm grateful to have met Beth. She believes that if things work out, we can make a positive impact."

"Beth, huh?" Elisa narrowed her eyes playfully. "Should I be jealous?"

Jackie chuckled. "She's the literary agent I mentioned to you."

"Ah, right," Elisa nodded, pretending to recall the information. "By the way, I've read your story."

Jackie's eyes lit up. "Really?"

Elisa smiled. "It's beautiful."

"Do you agree to publish it?"

"Well, it's a good story, but –"

"I hate the word 'but.'"

Elisa gave Jackie a somber look, carefully choosing her words. "I know you have high hopes, but honestly, our society isn't ready for this story. I appreciated it because I was there, and I know you. However, most people may perceive it differently – as something scandalous, filled with sins and inappropriate behavior. It could potentially tarnish your reputation as a lawyer."

Jackie locked eyes with Elisa. "I understand that it may not resonate with everyone. I wrote it for women who feel flawed but are seeking redemption. I aim to help them stop punishing themselves for their mistakes or imperfections."

"It's a noble intention, my dear. I just worry about the potential backlash. People might react unpredictably. If someone were to discover our relationship, we could risk losing everything."

"Are you certain there are no other options?" Jackie inquired, her hand moving to unbutton her shirt.

What a manipulative move! As always, it was effective. Elisa gazed at Jackie, unable to tear her eyes away from her beloved partner. "Well, I believe you should consider changing some names for our safety. After that, it should be good to go."

Filled with excitement, Jackie leaped off her chair and onto Elisa's lap, enveloping her in a tight hug. "I knew you would agree to publish it."

"I adore everything about you," Elisa said, brushing a strand of raven hair from Jackie's cheek. "And I have a present for you."

"You've already given me the best present – your support."

"This is the real one." Elisa revealed the pendant from beneath the napkin, allowing it to catch the flickering candlelight.

Jackie eyed her suspiciously. "A new chain? Isn't it expensive?"

"You are priceless," Elisa said, fastening the chain around Jackie's neck and admiring the way it looked on her. "And don't concern yourself with the cost. I have a promising new case that will cover our expenses."

"A new case?" Jackie smiled. "That sounds intriguing."

"We may have an undercover operation soon, so you can assist Urchin and me, just like in the good old days."

"I would love it," Jackie said, touching the jewelry. "And as for your present, I won't take it off to ensure I won't lose you."

"Whatever comes our way, I want you to know – I'll always stand by you, regardless of what others may say."

Jackie relaxed and kissed her.

Elisa's hands enveloped her back, delicately tracing along her spine. As the shirt dropped to the floor, she leaned in to nuzzle Jackie's breasts, breathing in the sweet scent of her skin. Elisa found solace in this intoxicating aroma, particularly after a taxing day at work. It served as the perfect antidote to daily stresses.

Jackie gently caught her hands. "I think I need to shower first."

"I can join you."

She smiled mischievously and rose from her seat. Elisa followed her to the compact shower room, where they could revel in the warmth of the water, the suds, and each other.

5

The Secret of Copper

Elisa and Urchin entered the spacious office, now illuminated by the bright morning sunlight. Walter Mills sat at his desk, diligently filling in the blanks on his report. Having recently been promoted to the position of lieutenant after successfully apprehending a notorious criminal gang, he now found himself buried in paperwork.

He looked up, his blue eyes meeting Elisa's. "Welcome to the team!"

"Glad to be a part of this investigation," Elisa replied with a smile.

Setting his pen aside, Walter gestured for Elisa to take a seat in front of him. Urchin settled into a nearby chair. Handing a stack of report papers to Urchin, Walter said, "Here. Yesterday, that girl Maya visited a small jewelry store and purchased five pounds of copper."

Elisa gritted her teeth. If only she had known that Maya would squander all her money, she would never have given it to her! Turning to Walter, she asked, "Why would they need that metal?"

"That's a good question, which is why I've called in an expert to analyze it," Walter replied.

The door swung open, and Edward, a young man with hazel eyes framed by round glasses, entered the room. A recent graduate of The Guardian Academy, Edward now worked at the Guardian House as an engineer, possessing a rare and valuable Gift that made him an expert in his field.

Edward nodded in greeting before turning his attention to Walter. "Lieutenant, may I proceed with my report?"

"Please do," Walter replied. "I hope you have some good news for us."

"Not exactly," Edward began, gesturing with his hands as he spoke. "As you're aware, this metal is commonly used in power cuffs to block magic channels. However, the magic does not disappear; it simply circulates continuously within the cuffs, unable to escape the wearer's wrists. Interestingly, this technology is not exclusive to guardians; it's also utilized by kidnappers and human traffickers. They use tight copper bracelets to prevent their victims from using magic."

"Do you mean to say that Incapables could potentially abduct our people?" Walter inquired, his brow furrowed in concern.

Edward shrugged. "It's a possibility. In fact, copper serves various purposes. Some rituals establish a stable connection between mages, even across distances. For instance, two mages sitting at opposite ends of a park could hold onto the ends of a copper wire and exchange their Lights or collaborate on a spell. This ritual was employed during a past conflict – multiple mages positioned in different parts of the town center held onto the wires to create a protective shield for the citizens."

"Incapables lack the ability to use magic in such a manner," Walter remarked. "That's why we call them 'Incapables.' But this situation poses a serious threat, and we must locate them as soon as possible to prevent potential kidnappings and other crimes."

"Agreed," Edward concurred, taking a seat and preparing for the upcoming brainstorming session.

All eyes turned to Walter as he stood up and walked over to the window. The morning frost had melted, leaving only bare, unsightly branches scraping against the glass. "Any suggestions on how we can apprehend them?" he inquired.

Elisa turned to Urchin. "You mentioned earlier that you tracked them but were unable to capture their leader. Why don't we attempt to follow them together?"

"Unfortunately, the physical limitations of my Invisibility spell restrict me to forty minutes, and if I have a companion, this duration is halved," Urchin explained. "Afterward, I'm left drained and physically exhausted. Pursuing them in such a state wouldn't work."

"I understand," Elisa replied, shifting uneasily in her chair. "And I assume that the Searching spell would be ineffective since they lack magical abilities."

"Exactly," Walter confirmed. "Otherwise, apprehending them would be a walk in the park."

Elisa turned to Edward with a thoughtful expression. "What if we were to use the Searching spell on an object rather than a person?"

Edward scratched his nose in contemplation. "What do you have in mind?"

Leaning back in her chair, Elisa recounted a story from her past. "Once, my aunt misplaced a family heirloom – her wedding ring. She enlisted the help of a witch to cast a Searching spell, which led her to a friend's house where it was discovered that the woman had stolen the ring."

Walter slammed his palm down on the table. "That's a fascinating tale for a gathering of women. Let's focus on our current situation, shall we?"

Elisa sighed. "Sir, I told you it only because I propose giving the Incapable girl a personal item, which we can then use to locate her and the others she works with."

"I see your point," Edward replied, his interest piqued. "I believe I can arrange that."

Urchin interjected with a skeptical expression. "How can we ensure that the girl won't trade the item for copper?"

"She won't," Elisa confidently asserted, capturing the attention of everyone in the room. She paused for a moment, relishing the anticipation before revealing her plan. "Because I'll give her something she won't part with – a new coat."

Urchin furrowed his brow. "We need a personal belonging to conduct the search spell. A new coat won't suffice."

"Have you ever heard the legend of the Trojan horse?" Elisa posed. "The coat will serve as our 'horse,' concealing the item in its inner pocket. We can stitch it securely, so she won't know she's been tracked."

Urchin fell silent, while Walter and Edward regarded Elisa with newfound admiration. She had just secured a pivotal role in the investigation, and failure was not an option. Unfortunately, luck had always been a fickle companion for her.

6

A Decision

Jackie pressed her forehead against the cold glass wall that separated a corridor from a large hall in the female shelter. The room was now occupied by women sitting in a circle on a lush carpet, surrounded by pillows of various shades and colors. Jackie quickly spotted Carrie, who was standing by the window, staring down at her feet as if they were the only thing of interest. The daylight made her neatly braided hair shine.

One of the women in the circle, a red-haired woman with dark blue eyes, picked up a plush teddy bear, indicating that it was her turn to speak. Her thin fingers squeezed the toy's head, causing it to shrink under her grip. She spoke in a confident voice, sharing her experience. "Like many of you, I was forced into this shelter. At that time, I was torn apart by grief and guilt. My newborn child died due to my neglect. I gave birth in December, and the following month, my child developed pneumonia.

"I blamed myself for taking long outdoor walks, believing that fresh air would benefit my child. However, I was terribly wrong. The cold air was too harsh for the baby, and it ultimately led to his death. I was advised to seek forgiveness, and I tried to obtain it from those I believed I had let down. Little did I know, I needed to forgive myself."

Carrie chuckled, drawing attention to herself.

"What's funny?" the red-haired woman asked, puzzled.

"It's not funny. It's selfish," Carrie said, shaking her head in disapproval. "If you do something wrong, you face the consequences. That's the Divine law, but you're too scared to confront it."

The woman paused, refuting Carrie's statement. "That's not true. I was prepared to face any consequences of my neglect. I was willing to accept punishment. I was only afraid to ask for Divine forgiveness. It was the most terrifying thing I've ever done in my life."

The other women in the circle nodded in agreement, prompting Carrie to move closer.

"It took me weeks to gather the courage," the red-haired woman continued. "I was afraid that I didn't deserve forgiveness. I knew my guilt was overwhelming, and I felt unworthy of seeking peace. However, I also understood that it wasn't my place to determine the course of my life. Life and death are in Her hands, and we can only be guided by Her Light. So, I went to the cathedral and sought Divine guidance."

Carrie nervously crumpled the hem of her dress. "What happened next?"

"One day, as I walked along the lake, I came across a fish lying on the sand. It was barely moving, almost lifeless. Without hesitation, I picked it up and gently returned it to the water, watching it disappear beneath the shimmering surface," the woman recounted, her dark-blue eyes filled with warmth. "In that moment, I had an epiphany. Yes, I may have made a grave mistake, but my life was not over. Perhaps I wasn't a perfect wife or mother, but I could dedicate the remainder of my days to doing good instead of dwelling on my past failures. I could learn from my shortcomings and use my experiences to assist other women in finding a way to take better care of their children and themselves. And so, I embarked on a journey to study medicine and became a doctor."

Carrie let out a heavy sigh and lowered her gaze.

"Today, I came to share my journey." The woman released the plush bear, allowing it to come to a rest at her feet. "I shared it because I have faith that She has a purpose for each of us. While the trials I faced may have been harsh, they have shaped me into the person I am today. All I had to do was ask. Ask, and She will guide you towards the right path. All you need is to have faith in Her wisdom and compassion."

Jackie lingered behind a pillar as the session concluded, allowing the women to pass through the corridor without noticing her. She was someone who had turned their lives upside down, so she preferred not to disrupt their peace. Today, one of the women lingered behind, and her soft footsteps came to a halt beside Jackie. Turning her head, Jackie found herself face to face with Beth, the red-haired woman.

"How did you like my speech?" Beth inquired, her blue eyes twinkling as she revealed a cunning smile.

"Well, I almost believed it," Jackie teased. "But seriously... Why did you fabricate being a doctor?"

Beth adjusted a lock of her copper hair. "Well, perhaps it didn't actually happen to me... But when I came across that story, I found it so beautiful. Today, I simply pretended it was my own."

Jackie let out a sigh, unable to argue with Beth. Despite Beth's lack of sincerity on this particular day, she possessed a persuasive quality that benefited the women in the room. Recognizing the value of this trait within their small community, Jackie decided it would be impolite to call out this harmless deception. "I'm glad you enjoyed taking on that role."

"I truly did," Beth replied with a charming smile. "I could do it again without any issue."

"I believe there's no need for that."

"There's always a need for good stories," Beth asserted, meeting Jackie's gaze. "You see, in times of change, we need each other."

"I understand," Jackie replied, casting a glance towards the empty corridor. With a new session about to begin, it was best to leave before they were noticed together. "Let's not discuss this here."

They strolled along the corridor, which had been freshly painted in a soft beige hue and adorned with pots and flowers. Though the flowers were not currently in bloom, the touches of greenery added a pleasant aesthetic to the surroundings.

At the end of the corridor was the door to Jackie's office, where she stored all the case files for the women residing in the shelter. The door was equipped with a smart lock – a metal rectangle positioned beneath the doorknob. Jackie raised her palm, allowing her blue Light to seep through her fingertips and form a ball. She then applied it to the lock, causing it to click open.

"So, how is your manuscript coming along?" Beth inquired impatiently as they entered the office.

"Actually, I have some good news for you," Jackie replied, her expression filled with joy. "I spoke with Elisa, and she agreed –"

"I can't believe it!" Beth interjected, her bony fingers clutching her shoulders. "Then I'll send it for printing tonight."

"Hold on." Jackie took a step back to create some distance between them. "We need to make a few changes before proceeding."

"What changes?" Beth questioned, furrowing her brow. "This story is flawless."

Jackie's heart pounded loudly in her chest. She was reluctant to cause confusion or delay the project, but she also had to prioritize Elisa's safety, as her private life was at the core of the story. Taking a seat on a soft chair, she waited for Beth to settle on a comfortable sofa.

"We need to consider changing the names," Jackie stated.

Beth gave her a weary look. "Okay, let's clarify the distinction between a fictional story and a memoir. In the case of fiction, readers view the characters and think, 'Wow, that would be great to experience, but it's not feasible in real life. Just a whimsical tale for naive girls.' However, in the case of a memoir, people perceive a true story that happened to a real person, which can truly inspire them."

Jackie lowered her gaze. "I understand. But it's still too risky for us."

"Risky?!" Beth scoffed. "This is the nature of new ideas and beliefs – they often require sacrifice to come to fruition. You have the potential to be a trailblazer, a woman who doesn't just talk about human rights and freedoms. You are the one who fought for your right to be a lawyer and to love whomever you choose. It all happened because you had the courage to leave behind your past prejudices. Now, it's time to share your incredible story with the world."

"I suppose I need to speak to Elisa again," Jackie said apologetically.

"Why?" Beth almost moaned. "You said she agreed."

"But it was just a verbal agreement between us. She agreed because she believed I would make it safe for both of us."

"Verbal is sufficient. We're good."

Jackie shook her head. "No, it's not right to proceed without discussing it with her. She won't forgive me if I go ahead without her consent. I believe I can find a way to persuade her eventually."

Beth placed her hand on her chest. "Ah, Jackie, you're a truly kind person, and I hate to tell you this, but Elisa may not be as trustworthy as you believe."

Jackie blinked. "What do you mean?"

Instead of responding, Beth rose from her seat and made her way to the door, searching for her coat. It was a long black woolen coat, likely an expensive one. Her hand delved into one of the large pockets, retrieving a milky-white memory crystal. Inside, a yellow energy emitted a recorded message, gleaming brightly. "Elisa approached me yesterday and attempted to bribe me to terminate our publishing agreement. It was quite a shock, especially considering how much faith you have in her. She simply doesn't want to jeopardize her career over what she deems a 'silly book.'"

Jackie sat in stunned silence, struggling to process this revelation about the woman she loved most. *No, Elisa would never do that. Why is Beth feeding me such a distressing lie?*

"I know this must be incredibly difficult for you," Beth said softly. "At first, I couldn't believe she was serious, but she was quite insistent. Luckily, I always carry my memory crystal with me for interviews. When I remembered it in my pocket, I activated it and managed to record a portion of our conversation."

"You mean... You recorded your conversation with Elisa?" Jackie asked in disbelief.

"Yes. I knew you wouldn't believe me without evidence," Beth replied, placing the crystal on the desk in front of Jackie. "Would you like to hear it?"

Jackie nodded, her heart heavy with anticipation.

Beth touched the crystal with her fingertips, and Elisa's voice filled the room.

"It's for Jackie."

"She is a special one, isn't she?" Beth's voice asked.

"Absolutely." The sound of rustling clothes followed. *"Can you help me with that? I want everything to look spotless."*

"Of course," Beth replied. *"Let's see what I can do about it."*

The recording was abruptly cut off by the squeak of the door. Beth turned off the crystal. "I'm truly sorry that you had to see this side of her."

"I don't understand," Jackie murmured, hugging her shoulders as goosebumps formed on her skin. "If she truly believes my story is silly and too risky, why did she agree to publish it in the first place?"

Beth shrugged. "She lied to you, can't you see that? Elisa only pretended to agree because she didn't have the courage to confront you directly and hurt you. Instead, she wanted me to do it. She even suggested offering money as a way out."

Could Elisa really betray me like this? Jackie closed her eyes as the world seemed to spin around her. Just last night, Elisa had mentioned that money wasn't an issue as she embarked on a new investigation. She had even given Jackie an expensive gift. Was it an attempt to distract her? Her heart raced, on the verge of shattering into a million pieces.

Beth let out a heavy sigh. "I know this is incredibly difficult. But it's time for you to make a decision."

"What decision?" Jackie asked in a hoarse voice, her emotions in turmoil.

"To do what's best for you and leave Elisa behind." Her words sounded like a death sentence.

"What do you mean by that?"

Beth gave her a sorrowful look. "Jackie, you can continue living a lie or take a stand and demonstrate the worth of your story. Additionally, being apart from Elisa may ensure the safety of both of you – it's impossible to assess the state of your relationship if there isn't one."

Jackie blinked, struggling to process the weight of Beth's words. It was all too overwhelming. Shock seemed to be the only emotion she could grasp at the moment.

"Women in our society are often silenced," Beth said. "They accept abuse as normal and view suffering as noble. You were no different until you nearly lost everything. That's why your story is so important. It has the potential to inspire women to realize they deserve equal rights to men."

Jackie nodded. "I understand. I just need some time to figure out what to say to her."

Beth rose from her seat and donned her coat. "You have until Monday to make your decision."

"But that's only three days away!"

"Exactly," Beth replied, glancing at her reflection in the mirror before heading towards the door. "I'll be waiting for you at noon at the cafe where we first met. I hope you'll have good news to share."

7

A Price of Trust

Elisa worked for the next two days until late at Guardian House, preparing for the undercover operation. Their engineer, Edward, was occupied with developing a modified Searching spell in the laboratory. They discovered that ordinary personal belongings held insufficient energy, rendering it impossible to locate them using a Searching spell. In order for their plan to succeed, they required a heirloom.

That's why Walter brought a diamond ring that had belonged to his grandmother and was intended to be given to his future fiancée, a lovely woman he had met at an autumn ball. As Walter was on the verge of proposing, he constantly checked on Edward to ensure the jewelry remained undamaged. Edward grew weary of this constant attention, so he retreated to the lab and left Elisa and Urchin to manage Walter's mood swings.

On the evening of the second day, Edward emerged from the lab, clutching the gleaming ring in his hand. He requested Elisa to conceal it somewhere within the building, and she opted to hide it in the kitchen. Edward successfully located the ring using a Searching spell, prompting them to proceed with the operation without further delay.

It was a chilly November evening, with the first snow blanketing the streets like a thin white veil. Elisa strolled along the bustling trade street, attempting to blend in as a casual shopper. Approaching the glass doors of a jewelry store, she caught sight of her reflection - clad in a black coat, her golden curls cascading from under a woolen hat onto her shoulders. Her cheeks flushed from the cold, the faint scar on her face nearly imperceptible.

Elisa gently touched her cheek, feeling the roughness where the killer's knife had once grazed her skin. Grateful for the second chance at life she had been given, she had embraced her role as a guardian. Her life often took unexpected turns, leaving her wondering what tonight might hold in store.

As the door swung open, Maya emerged from the store, clad in the same worn coat that tugged at Elisa's heartstrings. Oddly enough, Maya's urgent need for warm clothing played into Elisa's mission.

Meeting Elisa's gaze, Maya's expression registered surprise. "Elisa?!"

She returned her greeting with a warm smile. "Hey there. What brings you here?"

"Nothing much, just browsing," Maya replied, casting a quick glance over her shoulder as she adjusted her scarf.

Elisa placed a hand over her heart, assuming the role of a caring mother figure. "Oh, my dear! You must be freezing!"

Maya flinched. "Just a bit. I'm sorry... I know you gave me money to buy warm clothes, but I ended up using it to buy food for my friends."

Food, indeed. As if you dined on copper. Elisa continued to weave her narrative. "It's alright, dear. Let me accompany you to the store, and we'll find you the perfect warm coat to keep you from catching a cold."

"You're so kind, but my brother... If he finds out you helped me, I'll be in trouble," Maya said, offering Elisa a sad smile.

Elisa waved her hand dismissively. "Don't fret over such trivial matters. Men can be clueless when it comes to fashion. We'll find something similar but warmer, and he'll never suspect a thing."

"Really?" Maya's eyes lit up with hope.

"I'm sure of it. And if he does happen to notice, just tell him you 'borrowed' it," Elisa suggested with a wink.

Maya's expression turned eager. "Alright, then."

Elisa reached out her hand, and Maya took it. It felt strange to be in such close proximity to an Incapable. Despite the smudge of dirt on Maya's cheek and her worn-out attire, Elisa couldn't bring herself to view her as a cursed being. To Elisa, Maya was simply a girl in need of guidance, akin to a younger sister.

It was difficult to envision how Maya would react when Elisa inevitably betrayed her trust. As a guardian, it was her duty to deceive criminals in order to ultimately capture them. Elisa sighed, reflecting on how Jackie had opted for a different career path. It was for the best because Jackie had always detested these manipulative games.

Jackie gazed at the open sales journal in the store, her hands twisting the pencil in a nervous manner. It had been two days since her emotional encounter with Beth, yet she had not found the opportunity to speak with Elisa. The love of her life was consumed with preparations for the undercover operation, and now Jackie found herself participating in it, assuming the role of a salesperson in the store.

Playing this part came naturally to her; the real challenge lay in maintaining a facade of normalcy and concealing the weight of the heart-wrenching decision she would have to make the following morning.

"Are you alright?" Urchin's voice broke through her reverie, startling her. Somehow, he had managed to approach her unnoticed and now stood on the opposite side of the counter, holding a cardboard box in his hands.

"I'm fine," Jackie replied, forcing a smile. "What have you brought?"

"Our secret weapon," he grinned, placing the box in front of her. Together, they opened it and revealed the softest blue coat Jackie had ever held.

Jackie pressed the coat against her cheek, relishing its plushness. "I wish I could afford something like this."

"Well, then, you should choose a life partner who spends money wisely," Urchin said jokingly.

His words pierced Jackie like a dagger. Despite their breakup, she and Urchin had maintained an amicable relationship. He often teased her about her connection with Elisa, but she had never taken offense until now. Jackie had to avert her gaze to conceal the tears welling up in her eyes.

"Jackie?" Urchin's touch on her shoulder startled her.

Without uttering a word, she hurried to the storage room and retrieved an empty hanger for the coat. Clutching it to her chest, she took a deep breath, attempting to regain her composure. Counting to ten always helped calm her nerves. *One, two, three...*

As Jackie emerged from the storage room, Urchin assisted her in displaying the coat prominently on the front rack, ensuring it caught Elisa's attention as she escorted an Incapable girl inside. Glancing out the window, Jackie noted the encroaching darkness. Their guests would arrive any moment.

"I'm so sorry," Urchin said softly.

She turned to face him. "For what?"

"I apologize for my joke. I didn't realize it struck a nerve," Urchin said, offering her a sympathetic look. "If you ever need anything, whether it's financial assistance or advice, I'm here to help."

"And what advice would you offer me?" Jackie retorted. "To end things?"

His eyes widened in surprise. "Is it that serious?"

She averted her gaze, feeling remorse for her abrupt words. "I'm not sure."

"Then talk to me about it."

She sighed. Urchin possessed a knack for deciphering emotions through body language and had a deep understanding of her. It was challenging to conceal her concerns from him. "Thank you for the offer, but I think we'll manage."

He nodded. "Alright. Just remember, I'm here if you need to talk."

"I appreciate that," she replied with a faint smile.

"Let's change the topic," Urchin suggested. "Can you guess why it was so effortless for us to adapt to working here?"

Jackie surveyed the small shop, which was now empty and on the verge of closing for the day. The seller had simply handed her a uniform shirt and provided instructions on how to maintain sales records as they carried out their mission.

"That's an easy one. You mentioned being a guardian and needing to utilize this location," Jackie deduced.

"Nope. Revealing our identities as guardians could jeopardize the entire mission."

"Then how did you arrange that?"

Urchin strolled through the hall, relishing the chance to elucidate the intricate details he had meticulously crafted. "I assumed the role of a lazy, affluent young man seeking to prove his ability to work hard and be independent of his father. I offered the shop owner a sum of money to allow me to work for a few hours before closing, citing my father's imminent visit to make a significant purchase."

Jackie applauded his ingenuity. "How clever! And now we'll 'sell' the coat you've just brought."

"Exactly." Urchin nodded. "Assuming everything goes according to plan."

"It will," Jackie assured him. "But what about me? How did you explain my presence here?"

"Oh, that was simple. I mentioned that you have prior sales experience, so I needed your assistance with customer service and maintaining sales records to prevent any mishaps."

Jackie's smile widened. Despite being a lawyer now and giving her all in that role, she couldn't deny missing the thrill of detective work at times.

"Furthermore," Urchin added, "While you were overseeing things here, I took this coat to the cafe at the corner, where Edward placed the ring inside the inner pocket. He discreetly stitched it to ensure it wouldn't be discovered immediately."

"Great job!"

The glass doors swung open, causing a small bell to chime above them. They exchanged nods and turned to welcome the new arrivals.

As anticipated, Maya was absolutely enamored with the soft blue coat featuring a high collar. She twirled in front of the mirror, her curly brown hair cascading over her left shoulder as she slid her hands into the wide pockets, relishing the feel of the fabric.

Jackie circled around Maya, ensuring that the girl didn't stumble upon the discreetly stitched inner pocket where the ring was concealed. Thankfully, Maya was too caught up in her excitement to scrutinize the coat too closely.

"How do you like it?" Jackie inquired.

"I absolutely love it!" Maya smiled. "I just hope it's not too expensive."

"I believe we can offer a discount for your sister," Jackie suggested, winking at Elisa.

"Thank you so much," Elisa responded, placing her hand over her heart.

Jackie couldn't help but marvel at how convincingly Elisa played her role, as if she hadn't attempted to negotiate with her literary agent behind her back. Determined not to let her emotions sour the mission, Jackie redirected her focus to Maya. "You can wear it right now."

"Really?" Maya fluttered her eyelashes.

"Of course," Elisa replied with a gentle smile. "I'll take care of the rest, alright?"

Maya embraced her tightly. "Thank you so much, Elisa!"

Elisa patted her shoulders. "No problem."

With a smile, Maya waved goodbye and hurried towards the exit door.

Once Maya had left, Jackie made the necessary entries in the sales journal, and together with Urchin, they closed the shop.

Elisa awaited them outside, her face invigorated by the frosty air and her eyes gleaming with the thrill of a true detective. "Let's go, guys. Our team is waiting for us," she announced.

Urchin nodded, and the group strolled along the street together. Edward and Walter were already at the nearby cafe, ready to embark on the final phase of their mission – uncovering the intentions of the Incapables.

8

Untold Secrets

Elisa led the team consisting of Edward, Walter, Urchin, and Jackie. As they walked, she held a rope with the flying crystal. Activated Searching spell made it shimmer with a bright blue light and float in the direction of the Northern suburbs. As Edward had explained earlier, the regular Searching spell wasn't stable, so he had placed it into the crystal. Now, they had to follow it to find the ring.

The crystal led them to the spacious backyard of an abandoned factory, indicating that the Incapable kids were hiding somewhere inside. The crystal began blinking at the rusted metal doors, prompting Elisa to stop.

Edward rubbed his palms and remarked, "Here we are. They must be really close.

Walter, Jackie, and Urchin looked around, scanning the area. The old building loomed over them in silence, its empty dark windows appearing lifeless except for one on the second floor, which was illuminated by shimmering candlelight.

Elisa turned to Walter. "Lieutenant Mills, we have arrived. What's our next move?"

Walter took a step back and scratched his chin, deep in thought. "There shouldn't be many of them, so we'll split up. Urchin, you'll come with me first and make us invisible. Edward, you'll follow us, staying several steps behind to provide cover in case of danger."

Elisa raised her hand, and violet sparkles of electricity crackled between her fingers. "With all due respect, Lieutenant Mills, I can better protect you."

"That's precisely why I need you here – to safeguard our mind reader and shield her if these rats attempt to escape through the backdoor," Walter explained. "I can't leave two people with mental Gifts outside."

Elisa nodded. "Understood."

Jackie embraced Urchin. "Please, be careful."

"I will," he replied with a smile.

Elisa frowned. It wasn't that Urchin's behavior ever bothered her – this guy had once been in love with Jackie and always looked out for her, even after their breakup. There was something odd about Jackie. She had been acting strangely in the past few days since getting involved in the new investigation with the Incapable kids. She had become distant, as if preoccupied with something serious. Knowing Jackie well, Elisa could tell when she was deeply worried and keeping it to herself. Perhaps now was the ideal moment to have a conversation and uncover what was troubling her.

Walter gestured for the guys to enter the building, leading the way as they left the front door partially open. The backdoor was located on the side of the factory, prompting Elisa and Jackie to walk to the corner of the building to keep an eye on all the exits.

"Well, at least we'll have this time together," Elisa remarked with a smile as they came to a stop.

Jackie shrugged and walked over to the nearest tree, its bark now glowing with a pale lilac light. Just like Jackie, nature was fragile and beautiful, capable of enhancing even the most unattractive surroundings.

Leaning against the tree trunk, Jackie gazed at the illuminated window as if work was her sole focus at that moment.

Sensing something amiss, Elisa decided to address the issue directly. "What's wrong?"

Avoiding eye contact, Jackie withdrew her hands into her coat pockets. "Nothing."

"Then kiss me," Elisa suggested.

"Now?" Jackie looked puzzled. "We're in the middle of our mission."

"Exactly. I need it for luck," Elisa explained, moving closer and placing her hand on the rough tree trunk above Jackie's head.

Jackie's emerald eyes reflected pure disappointment as she slid down and stepped away from Elisa's embrace.

Elisa turned to her, puzzled. "Okay, I'm not sure what I did wrong, but whatever it is, please tell me."

Exhaling a cloud of vapor into the frosty air, Jackie retorted, "So you're just going to pretend like nothing happened?!"

Elisa stood in silence, her mind racing through the events of the past few days. Nothing stood out – everything seemed normal, although she realized she may have been preoccupied and not given their relationship the attention it deserved. "Um... Can I have a hint?"

"A hint?" Jackie gave her a dirty look. "I know the truth. You never wanted me to publish that story."

"I do want it published. And if I recall correctly, we discussed it and reached an agreement."

"And yet, you've ruined everything," Jackie accused, her expression stern.

Confused, Elisa furrowed her brow. "What do you mean?"

Jackie's glare intensified. "I know you met with Beth."

Elisa swallowed, trying to recall the significance of that name from their past conversations. "Beth?"

"My literary agent," Jackie clarified. "And stop pretending you can't remember her name!"

"Darling, I swear I've never met this woman in my life," Elisa said, attempting to ease the tension. However, her words seemed to only agitate Jackie further.

"You swear, then..." Jackie's tone was grave.

"Yes."

The loud bang interrupted their conversation, causing both Elisa and Jackie to turn their heads towards the windows. Heavy smoke and flames billowed out from the broken glass, indicating a fire inside the building. Something had clearly gone wrong, and they needed to keep a close watch on the exit doors.

"Crap!" Jackie muttered, darting towards the front door.

Elisa moved to stop her, but it was too late – Jackie had already vanished into the building. Unable to leave the back door unguarded, Elisa conjured electricity balls in each hand and pressed herself against the wall, ready and waiting.

Peering cautiously from the corner, Elisa spotted the silhouettes of two young men making their escape towards the forest. They were too far away for her to attempt to catch them. *Did they see Jackie and me?* Elisa wondered. *They must have slipped out through the window while we were distracted by our argument.*

Frustrated, Elisa shook her head. While it wasn't ideal, there was still a possibility that some Incapables remained inside the building. Elisa ventured into the backyard, her path illuminated by the glowing lightning balls in her hands, casting a moon-like light around her.

As the door swung open, Maya emerged, her eyes widening in surprise. "Elisa?"

"Hey," Elisa greeted, lowering her hands to appear less intimidating. "What are you doing here?"

Maya glanced nervously towards the forest before turning back to Elisa. "These guardians found us. Eric told me to hide, but I got too scared."

"Wait," Elisa paused, a realization dawning on her. "Eric is your brother?"

"Yes." Maya nodded, oblivious that she had just provided Elisa with a crucial piece of information.

"Did he leave you alone here?"

Tears welled up in Maya's eyes. "I don't know what to do if they catch him. I have no one left in this world. Only him!"

Elisa's heart ached at Maya's words. She dropped the lightning balls, allowing them to burst on the ground before embracing the girl. Maya's shoulders trembled as Elisa gently stroked her hair. "It's okay – he managed to escape."

"Really?" Maya asked through her sobs.

"Yes. I saw them running towards the forest," Elisa explained.

Taking a step back, Maya looked at Elisa with confusion. "Why are you helping me?"

Elisa gazed up at the waxing gibbous moon, seeking a fitting response. The moon seemed to offer a crooked smile in return. What could she possibly say to Maya? The truth was, Elisa had to let the girl go, as Maya possessed a ring that could potentially lead them to the Incapable lawbreakers. Mainly to Eric, who was a key figure in this investigation.

Throughout her time as a guardian, Elisa had apprehended numerous criminals, but this particular case tugged at her soul. It was agonizing to have to separate Maya from her only sibling, but it was her duty. To begin with, she needed to earn Maya's trust.

"I'm helping you because I understand your grief. When I was eleven, I became an orphan," Elisa revealed, her voice tinged with emotion.

Maya broke down in tears. "I don't have anyone but Eric."

Elisa regarded Maya with a remorseful expression. "Listen, let's make a deal. I'll allow you to go and search for your brother. He should be somewhere nearby. If anything goes wrong afterward, you can always find me, and I'll help you."

Maya nodded in gratitude, stepping back before rushing forward to embrace Elisa. "Thank you so much."

The voices of the guardians could be heard from the open windows, indicating their proximity. "Hurry," Elisa urged.

Maya nodded once more before darting off towards the glowing trees. Elisa turned and made her way back to the front yard.

Inside the building, Jackie hurried upstairs, the thick smoke making it difficult to breathe. She pulled her scarf up over her nose to filter the air, but the acrid black smoke still stung her eyes, causing tears to well up and blur her vision. Despite the discomfort, Jackie pressed on, her determination overriding the urge to retreat. She moved cautiously, relying on her sense of hearing to guide her through the smoke-filled environment.

Her heart felt heavy in her chest, torn between the lingering hurt from Elisa's deception and the concern for her friends who were on their way to apprehend the Incapables. Unable to change the situation with Elisa, Jackie focused on her mission – it was something she could control and set right.

Ascending the stairs, Jackie trusted her instincts, sensing that something was amiss. Even if Walter and the team hadn't yet captured the criminals, she expected that they would have fled the building by now.

A scream echoed from behind the wall, prompting Jackie to move closer. Someone had locked the double doors from the outside using a broomstick, wedging it through both handles after the guardians had entered. The frantic sound of kicking against the door indicated someone was trapped inside, desperate to escape.

"Pull back!" Jackie shouted, and the kicking ceased. She swiftly removed the broomstick, allowing the door to swing open wide. Heavy smoke obscured her vision, but she recognized Edward's voice. She grabbed his hand, and they made their way downstairs together.

Once outside, Jackie finally took a deep, refreshing breath. Edward held her hand, while Walter supported her with his elbow, carrying the unconscious Urchin. Both men coughed heavily as they slowly regained their senses.

In the yard, they laid Urchin on a bench, and Jackie leaned over him to check his pulse. His breathing was slow but steady, indicating that he was alive.

"What happened there?" Jackie asked, her voice weak from the intensity of the situation.

Edward looked up at the raging flames. "They set the lab on fire. We entered, and I managed to grab one of their details. The next moment, there was an explosion. I believe it was a bomb."

He coughed into his fist, spitting out black saliva onto the ground. "Urchin was too close, and he suffered the most."

Jackie wasted no time and began casting a spell, her blue Light shimmering over Urchin's head as she whispered a Life-supporting incantation. As her energy flowed into his chest, she felt a wave of dizziness wash over her, causing her to lean over the bench for support.

Edward smiled faintly. "You two always had this connection."

"What connection?"

Edward shrugged. "When you share your Light with someone, you kind of enter each other's personal space, and your bond deepens."

Jackie's gaze shifted to Urchin, her heart stirring with a sudden memory. She recalled the night they shared their first kiss. Back then, Urchin had bravely defended her in a fight, and after that, she had used her Light to heal his wounds. The memory then led to them moving to his bedroom...

Being with Urchin had always felt right to Jackie. She never viewed their connection as a mistake, only as a valuable experience. Unlike Elisa, Urchin had always been honest with her, and she appreciated that about him. Gently stroking his cheek to remove the black marks, she felt the pleasant tickle of his light bristle against her fingertips.

Lost in her thoughts, Jackie blinked and shook her head, trying to clear her mind from the confusion and shock of the recent events.

"You two have a strong bond," Edward chimed in, looming over her. As an engineer, he claimed to see invisible connections between people, and he seemed to relish in his insight.

"Edward, do you know why some people lie to the ones they love?" Jackie asked.

He shrugged. "Humans are wired that way. We lie, thinking we're protecting someone, but in the end, it often causes more harm."

"That's true," Jackie agreed.

The two fell into a contemplative silence, the only sounds being their breathing and the crackling of the flames in the distance. With only the three of them near the bench, Lieutenant Walter went to send a Light signal to alert the guardians on duty for assistance. As he returned, Elisa walked back with him, joining the group.

Elisa looked at Jackie with a puzzled expression, so she removed her hand from Urchin's face.

"I shared my Light with Urchin," Jackie explained. "He should be feeling better now."

Walter nodded in approval. "Good job. The guardians should be here in five minutes. You girls can probably go."

Jackie hesitated, then firmly stated, "No." Her voice came out louder than intended, causing Elisa to flinch. She quickly lowered her voice. "I mean... I'll go to the hospital with Urchin."

Elisa sighed and turned to Walter. "What happened?"

"The Incapables set a trap, and the room was set on fire when we entered. They were trying to destroy whatever they were working on."

"What were they making?" Elisa inquired. "Does it have something to do with copper?"

Walter nodded in confirmation.

Edward smiled and pulled a small box from his pocket. "We managed to find this."

"What's that?" Elisa asked, puzzled.

Edward shrugged. "I'm not entirely sure, but from a quick glance, I can tell it's designed to capture waves from a distance."

Elisa furrowed her brow in confusion. "Waves? From the ocean?"

"No, it's more like capturing voices or messages. I'm not entirely sure, but I'll investigate further in my lab."

Walter nodded in agreement. "Just like you did with my ring."

"Exactly," Edward affirmed.

Walter's expression turned anxious. "By the way, where is my ring?"

Elisa glanced towards the corner of the building. "When I arrived, the suspects had already fled. However, I did encounter Eric's sister and decided to let her go. Hopefully, she will lead us to him."

Edward shook his head. "Searching spells have a limited range. If they move too far from the city, we won't be able to track them."

"We should pursue them now!" Walter said.

Elisa reasoned, "Without horses, it wouldn't be practical. We're slower than them on foot. Additionally, we can only use the Searching spell on Maya. If she becomes suspicious and discards the coat, we'll lose our only lead. It's better to wait for the Incapables to regroup and return to Middle Lake."

"Perfect. Like hell they'll come back," Walter grumbled in frustration.

Elisa reached into her pocket and retrieved the crystal with the Searching spell. It shimmered with a pale inner light, indicating that the connection was weakening.

"The connection is getting weaker," Edward observed. "But they must have returned to the city. After all, only the capital has enough shops where they can continue stealing copper. I'll keep an eye on this crystal. When the girl returns, I'll be alerted, and we can move in to make the arrest."

"Understood," Walter replied with a nod.

The sound of approaching horse hooves grew louder. Two guardians neared them and dismounted from their horses. One of them assisted Jackie in placing Urchin in a carriage, and they set off for the hospital, leaving the rest of the squad to continue their investigation.

9

A Voice from the Crystal

Elisa wandered along the corridor of the Guardian House in the early morning. Here, on the ground floor, the daylight was dim, and the walls were painted gray. Her mood wasn't any brighter. Last night, she had been waiting for Jackie to talk to her, but tiredness had taken over after midnight, and she had fallen asleep on the sofa. In the morning, she found Jackie napping in their bed and decided not to disturb her sweet dreams. The idea of waking her up didn't seem wise. Jackie had a busy night and needed to catch some sleep before starting her own work.

Why do our schedules always conflict? Elisa reached the doors of the lab and pushed them open with force. Edward was already inside, wearing his peculiar goggles. He was fully focused on a copper box he had discovered the previous night in the abandoned factory. Two transparent crystals were connected to the box by copper wires. Not wanting to interrupt his work, Elisa sat on the nearest chair and rested her cheek on her hand, watching him.

Edward wiped the sweat from his forehead and glanced at her. "Incredible. This thing is a real game-changer. This could potentially become one of the most revolutionary inventions in human history!"

Elisa raised her eyebrows. "Really? And how exactly will it help?"

He gave her a sly smile and removed his goggles, revealing two red circles around his eyes. With his disheveled hair, he looked like a mad genius struck by lightning. Elisa chuckled.

Edward handed her both crystals from the table. They were partially wrapped in copper wire, as if it were an essential component for this newly invented device. She twisted them in her hands. "Looks strange."

"I need you to charge them using your Light," he said.

Elisa complied with his request. She raised her palm, and her silver Light leaked from her fingertips, forming a ball. She then touched the crystals with her Light, and it seeped inside. The crystals shimmered and became clear again. "Ready. Now what?"

"I have already charged both crystals with my Light, which means they are attuned to our energies. This allows us to communicate with each other." He took one of the crystals and attached it to his ear using the wire. "Let's give it a try. Call me."

She cleared her throat and brought the crystal closer to her mouth. "Hello? Edward?"

He chuckled. "No, not like that. Allow me to demonstrate first. All you need to do is touch the crystal with your fingertips, like this." He touched his crystal and stepped back. "Then close your eyes and focus on the person you wish to communicate with. Visualize their Light."

"Can I speak to Jackie?" She asked with a hint of sadness.

"No, it must be someone who has charged the crystal. So, your only option is me," he replied, smiling playfully. "So, at this moment, I'm calling you." He closed his eyes. "Elisa. A rare shade of silver Light with golden sparkles. Hear my call." He raised his hand, mimicking a preacher delivering a grandiose speech.

Elisa was about to burst into laughter when the crystal in her hand suddenly began vibrating with green Light. "What on earth?"

"You see my Light, indicating that I'm calling you. You just need to touch it to establish the connection," Edward explained.

Elisa touched the crystal and brought it closer to her face. "Like this?"

"Exactly."

His voice resonated directly from the crystal, causing Elisa to almost drop it. She gazed at this marvel of science in awe, speechless as she listened to Edward's voice.

"Now, let's create some distance," he said, walking towards the corridor and closing the door behind him. "How is the sound now?"

"Very clear. But Ed, what does this mean? Can Incapables communicate like this... over a distance?"

"No, they lack Light," he replied, pausing to think. Elisa could hear his footsteps echoing in the corridor, followed by the creak of an opening door. "Oh, hi, Urchin."

"Hey," Urchin's voice sounded weak. Elisa felt a pang of sympathy for him – he had spent the night in the hospital and had returned as soon as he was discharged. She had intended to greet him with a cheerful 'Hi,' but his next words caught her off guard.

"Is Elisa there?" Urchin inquired.

"Yes, she's in the lab," Edward responded.

"Gee, can I avoid seeing her today?" Urchin's request made Elisa hold her breath.

Edward seemed to have forgotten about the magical crystal as he continued the conversation openly. "No, we are a team, so we must work together. Come on, it's been several years. Are you still upset with her because of Jackie?"

"It's not that. I spoke to Jackie last night, and she told me how Elisa betrayed her."

Elisa's eyes widened in shock. She almost asked for clarification but restrained herself, remaining silent and allowing Urchin to explain further.

"What happened?" Edward inquired.

"She bribed her literary agent to sabotage the book project," Urchin revealed.

Elisa gazed at her crystal in disbelief. The previous night, Jackie had accused her of meeting with her agent, which was somehow related to her manuscript. Where had these lies originated from?

The crystal blinked, and the Light faded. Perhaps Edward had finally realized that she might be listening in and decided to end the connection.

Nevertheless, Elisa had heard enough. She leaped from her chair and stared out the window, deep in thought. It was Monday morning, the time when Jackie typically worked at the shelter. Elisa contemplated paying her a visit there and confronting her about the situation. However, she doubted Jackie would be forthcoming with the truth. Alternatively, she could track down Jackie's agent and extract the truth from her. If only she knew when or where their next meeting was scheduled. Or even the agent's name. *Belle? Brie? Shit, if only I had paid more attention!*

Elisa had no doubt that Urchin knew how to locate the agent, so she considered enlisting his help to obtain this crucial information. It seemed like the most effective way to unravel the mystery.

The door swung open, and the guys entered the room. Urchin gave her a quick nod before turning to Edward. "Did you find out anything about the copper box?"

Edward placed the crystal on the desk, appearing hesitant. "Yes. Now, we understand how they can establish a connection. However, since they lack magic, it could involve a different form of energy. Perhaps electricity."

"Isn't electricity a form of magic?" Elisa pondered. "It's my Gift, in case you've forgotten."

Edward gave her a weary look. "No offense, but your grasp of science is lacking, like most guardians."

Urchin chuckled. "And Incapables are geniuses in it, huh?"

"Some of them are," Edward conceded. He walked over to his bookshelf and retrieved a thick manual. Flipping through the pages, he stopped at a diagram depicting a copper box similar to the one they had found, but with a slender rod attached to its side. "Here it is. He referred to it as a 'Radio.'"

"Radio?" They echoed in unison.

Edward nodded. "Yes. It's a method of communication that allows people to connect over a distance without relying on magic. Interestingly, this invention belongs to an engineer who lost his magical abilities during an extended stay on Death Island."

"Wait, he lived among us?" Elisa asked in disbelief.

"Yes." Edward nodded. "He wasn't a criminal. He was a laborer who suffered the loss of his magic while installing facilities in an area with a severe magnetic anomaly. Additionally, he had a family and agreed with the government not to have more children to prevent the birth of Incapables. Consequently, he was permitted to work in a laboratory where his expertise and skills were invaluable. He developed numerous inventions that could enhance the lives of Incapables like himself."

Elisa found herself intrigued by the engineer's story. In her experience, Incapables were typically relegated to menial labor roles and were often marginalized. She had never encountered someone who not only managed to lead a fulfilling life after losing their magic but also continued to work as an engineer, leaving behind a legacy of inventions. After meeting Maya, Elisa struggled to discern significant differences between mages and Incapables. Ultimately, both groups were composed of humans facing similar challenges.

"Jackie would be fascinated by this tale," Urchin remarked.

"Indeed, she would," Elisa concurred. "She genuinely cares about everyone, even outcasts."

Urchin fixed her with an intense gaze. "Do you realize how many people became Incapables due to accidents or because of the actions of Mercy House collectors?"

Elisa shrugged. "I imagine there are many. However, it may not be good for them to live among us."

"Well, why not?" Urchin countered. "As long as they abide by the law, I don't see any issue."

"You're correct," Edward remarked. "Their reputation is tarnished, though, and earning trust is a challenging task."

"And destroying it is all too easy," Elisa added.

"Precisely," Urchin agreed.

Elisa took a deep breath. No doubt, Urchin was intent on keeping his secret about Jackie. Confronting him would likely be futile, so she decided to appeal to his feelings for her girlfriend.

She circled around the desk and stood beside him. "Hey, Urch, I have a special surprise planned for Jackie today, and I could really use your help."

"Haven't there been enough surprises already?!"

"This one is different. I want to arrange a meeting with her agent to discuss something important."

He squinted at her. "And?"

"I would be grateful if you could assist me in finding out when and where their meeting will take place. I'm not privy to that information."

"Why would I know that?"

"Because you two spoke yesterday. Jackie tends to confide in you about such matters."

"Perhaps because I'm the only one who bothers to listen?" he suggested.

The weight of Urchin's words was like a punch to the gut. What stung the most was that he was right – he paid attention and remembered the important details about Jackie's life that Elisa had overlooked. "Please, Urch. You just need to distract Jackie on her way there. Just engage her in conversation on the street. I only need a minute with her agent, that's all."

"So, you trust me, huh? What if I decide to disobey and bring Jackie to your meeting? I can shield her with my Invisibility so she could learn something that would shatter her heart."

Elisa adopted a sorrowful expression. "Then you would ruin the surprise. I trust you wouldn't do that to her."

"Alright, let's do it, then," Urchin agreed.

Edward, who had been silently listening, now interjected, rubbing his hands together. "I'm glad you two have come to an agreement. It's crucial to address this 'betrayal' situation promptly."

Elisa furrowed her brow. "It's fine, Edward. You don't need to get involved."

Urchin gave Elisa a puzzled look. "So you're admitting to your betrayal?"

She hesitated, glancing around the room. The last thing she wanted to do was explain herself to Urchin, who had just agreed to help her.

Edward cleared his throat. "Alright, let's clarify things. Since I'm the only one without a conflict of interest, here's what I have." He walked over to the board, picked up a piece of chalk, and began drawing geometric shapes and lines, connecting them. "So, here we have Jackie," Edward pointed at the circle. "She alleges that Elisa bribed her literary agent."

"I never did that!" Elisa stated.

Edward nodded and pointed to the triangle. "And here is Elisa, who denies the accusation."

"Furthermore, I've never even met the agent in person," Elisa added.

Urchin scoffed. "Liar."

Edward drew a square in the center of the board, seemingly unfazed by the ongoing argument. "Allow me to remind you of the first rule of detective work. Before making accusations, we must identify all potential suspects and investigate them. Let's consider everyone involved and examine their motives. Now, let's focus on the agent... What's her name?"

Elisa furrowed her brow, trying to recall.

Urchin raised his hand. "Beth."

"Yes, Beth," Elisa confirmed, promising herself to remember it.

Edward dusted off his hands, clearing them of chalk residue. "Does Beth have any reason to deceive Jackie?"

"No," Urchin asserted. "Beth's primary goal is to assist Jackie in getting her story published. Additionally, she claims to possess a recording of Elisa's voice that incriminates her."

"That can't be true," Elisa objected. "I would remember if I had met her."

"But Jackie allegedly heard the recording herself!" Urchin countered.

Elisa's eyes widened in disbelief. "That's impossible!"

Edward raised his hand, making a point. "Quiet down, everyone! There must be a logical explanation for this."

"How about Elisa being a liar?" Urchin persisted.

Elisa turned to Edward, hoping he would see reason.

Edward shook his head. "I find that hard to believe."

"Why not?" Urchin asked.

"Well, if Elisa were lying, she wouldn't have suggested that you distract Jackie. It's clear she wants to uncover the truth after overhearing our conversation in the corridor."

Urchin regarded Elisa with suspicion. "So you were eavesdropping? But how? You were in the lab the whole time, and the walls are thick."

"Crystals," Elisa said.

"What?!"

"I'll explain that part later," Edward interjected. "For now, the crucial thing is to develop a viable theory and investigate it."

Elisa paced back and forth, deep in thought. "This Beth... She somehow stole my voice."

"Indeed," Edward acknowledged. "She may have used a Hypnotic spell on you, causing you to divulge information to her and subsequently forget about it."

"Any Hypnotic spell would dissipate within twenty-four hours," Urchin stated matter-of-factly. "Those under the influence of Hypnosis typically recall their actions but struggle to find a logical explanation for them."

Elisa massaged her temples. "I can't make sense of it. I don't even recall meeting her!"

Urchin let out a sigh. "Alright, you've piqued my curiosity. Let's head over there and investigate this case."

10

The Face of Truth

The cafe was almost empty, with only a few visitors sitting at small round tables, eating their lunch alone and reading books and newspapers. Elisa gazed out through the glass of a large window, her eyes coming to rest on a red-haired woman in a white sweater. The woman looked familiar, and Elisa felt they may have met before. *But when?*

The woman sipped her tea and glanced at the window, causing Elisa to quickly look away.

"It's her," Urchin said. "Are you ready to confront her?"

"I hope I'm not losing my mind," Elisa said, running her fingers through her hair. "I think I've seen this woman before, but I swear to Divine, I never discussed Jackie's book with her!"

"Are you sure?" Urchin narrowed his eyes. "How did she record your voice, then?"

Elisa paused. "Alright, if I ever talked about anything related to Jackie, she might have used a Forgetting potion."

"Which would make you forget the rest of the day," he said, giving her a skeptical look. "Have you experienced any memory-loss episodes recently?"

"No." Elisa shook her head. "What if she got me drunk?"

"When was the last time you drank alcohol?"

"Um... A couple of months ago. On your birthday. Wait, was she invited?"

"Apparently not. And even if she were there, I would remember that!"

Elisa moaned, feeling helpless. *Did I really bribe her and forget about it?* She would never come to such a conclusion, but something similar had already happened to her several years ago during an episode with taking Moondust. She hadn't touched a drop of it since rehab, but what if this drug had caused the brain damage that all the doctors had warned her about?

"Alright, let's calm down," Urchin said, handing her a snow-white memory crystal. Elisa took it with her numb fingers. "Just try to talk to her and record what she says. It's the only way to figure out the truth."

She nodded and tucked the crystal into her chest pocket. It was the scariest thing now – to face that woman and bring this investigation to a close. But she must do it because it was the only way to regain Jackie's trust, even if it meant uncovering something unsettling about herself and potentially being placed in the nearest asylum.

"Don't be scared," Urchin said. "I'll be nearby to help you."

She gave him a sad look. Would Urchin truly visit her in a hospital ward? She could envision herself lying in bed with vacant eyes and a drug-induced smile. Jackie and Urchin would come to visit her, attempting to bring her back to her senses. Elisa shook her head to dispel the image.

Unable to bear any more of this suspense, Elisa turned to enter the cafe through the glass door.

Approaching the red-haired woman, Beth, as she now recalled, Elisa took a seat in front of her.

Beth raised her dark-blue eyes, looking surprised. "Elisa?"

Elisa nodded silently.

"What are you doing here?" Beth asked.

Her mouth went dry, so Elisa emptied a glass of water in three gulps. She wiped her lips before speaking. "I know what you did to Jackie. I just want to know why you did it."

"And what have I done?" Beth gave her a small smile. "Just showed her your true intentions." She fidgeted, adjusting her expensive black coat that hung on the back of the chair. Her dark-blue silk scarf peeked out from the pocket. This scarf... it matched her eyes.

Elisa's breath caught as the memory hit her. It was a brief conversation she had with a sales associate when she entered a jewelry store to buy Jackie a gift. They exchanged a few words before Maya walked in, interrupting them.

Elisa clenched her fists. "You pretended to work in a jewelry store to record my voice. How pathetic."

Beth laughed. "So you finally recognized me. Very well."

Elisa exhaled a sigh of relief. It wasn't her memory issues after all. This woman had taken advantage of her, causing both her and Jackie to doubt everything they had worked so hard to build over the years. "Why did you do this to us?"

Beth shrugged and glanced around, ensuring that no one was eavesdropping. "Money, of course. You see, one publisher really liked the idea of a light erotica novel about two female guardian cadets who break the rules to be together."

"And you wanted to eliminate me so that Jackie would agree to publish it as revenge?"

"She wouldn't necessarily view it as revenge," Beth replied, taking a sip of her tea. "You see, she can be too kind at times. So I tried to convince her that explicit scenes would attract more young male readers to the story. Then, they would be inspired to support women like her."

"But that's nonsense."

"Of course," Beth agreed. "In fact, they usually skim through the plot to get to the sex scenes. As you know, selling explicit books is illegal. But this read provides a clever way to make money – it has a 'story' within the story."

Elisa twisted her glass in her hand. The memory crystal was in her inner pocket, activated and recording their conversation. It would provide her with all the evidence she needed. However, it was disheartening to receive such a blunt response. Deep down, she had always hoped for Jackie to succeed in everything she believed in, and she detested those who sought to tarnish her reputation like this. "Is there any chance of finding a more appropriate audience?"

Beth placed her empty cup on the table and rolled her eyes. "Honey, being an author is tough. It takes years to capture the reader's attention. People aren't very patient these days. This is the quickest route. Plus, we'll be well-compensated, and you'll receive your share."

"I don't need this money," Elisa said, giving Beth a disdainful look. "I believe that Jackie's story deserves more respect."

"You can believe whatever you want. I know how it works."

Elisa nodded and stood up. "I should go now."

"I hope you won't speak ill of me," Beth remarked. "I assume you wouldn't want to disappoint Jackie by revealing the truth about her prospects as an author."

Elisa hesitated. This was the last thing she wanted. Perhaps Beth's strategy wasn't that bad – I would let Jackie find some happiness from sharing her story. Maybe most people would only see their memoir as fodder for their sexual desires, but there would be someone who truly appreciated the tale of a woman who confronted domestic violence and triumphed. "Suppose you're right. However, you framed me. To continue our collaboration, you will need to clarify this misunderstanding to Jackie."

"No need. I've heard enough," Jackie's voice echoed from nowhere.

Elisa looked around in surprise.

Jackie materialized above Beth, clad in her black coat and wearing a somber expression. Her green eyes were as dark as the depths of a forest. "I no longer require your services, Beth."

Beth rose from her seat, but Jackie was already striding towards the glass doors. Elisa followed her out onto the street.

Outside, the bright sun bathed the snowy street in warmth. Jackie leaned against the wall, her face buried in her hands. It was evident she needed a moment to compose herself.

Elisa glanced back at the cafe. Urchin had dispelled his invisible shield and was now interrogating Beth. As a guardian, he could easily accuse her of gaslighting. Beth had fabricated evidence and manipulated Jackie for financial gain. They had all the evidence needed to have her arrested, provided Jackie was willing to testify as a victim.

Elisa deactivated her memory crystal, watching as it shimmered with an inner yellow light, preserving the evidence of Beth's confession. Her heart pounded loudly in her chest. What if Urchin was the one who truly deserved her? This thought had often crossed her mind, and she had tried to push it away until now. But it was becoming clear – unlike her, he was fully aware of everything happening in Jackie's life. He paid attention to all the details, while Elisa was often too focused on her work.

Approaching Jackie, Elisa placed her hands on her shoulders. Jackie looked up with tear-filled eyes. "I'm so sorry, Lissy. I don't know why I believed her. I should have talked to you before today..." Her voice quivered, and she began to cry.

"It's not your fault," Elisa reassured her, embracing her and allowing Jackie to bury her face in her shoulder. "Don't blame yourself. Anyone can be deceived like this. That's her job – manipulating your dreams for her own gain."

Jackie leaned back and locked eyes with Elisa. "It's not about her. I knew that these things often happen. After all, I'm a mind-reader."

"Did you read Beth?"

Jackie shook her head. "We signed a confidentiality agreement."

"Of course," Elisa grumbled.

"I mean... I understand how most people think. Everything she said about the readers is true."

"But if you knew that... Maybe you shouldn't terminate your publishing contract?" Elisa suggested.

"I have to. Don't you see? It nearly destroyed our relationship," Jackie's words struck Elisa like sharp needles. Jackie was never at fault for their distance, but she seemed to believe otherwise. "I was so consumed with your perceived need to protect me that I didn't truly communicate with you since Beth showed me the recording of your conversation! I was willing to reject you just to publish that story. I can't let it come between us anymore."

"Well, I would rather find another agent," Elisa said, wiping her cheek. "Someone trustworthy."

"I doubt they exist."

"We're not in a hurry. Whenever you find one, I'm confident you'll become a fantastic author and advocate for women."

"Do you truly believe in me?"

"Absolutely," Elisa replied, gently stroking her hair. "And you're right – I'm tired of letting our work come between us. Let's prioritize ourselves now."

"It's challenging with your job," Jackie pointed out.

"Nothing is impossible. Starting now, I'll take at least one day off each week to spend the entire day with you."

"For real?" Jackie's eyes widened, returning to their normal emerald hue.

"For real," Elisa confirmed with a smile. "And let's plan a little getaway to visit a dragon farm in Triville."

"Absolutely. It's a shame we've never been there together," Jackie agreed. "When should we go? In the summer?"

"How about the first week of December?" Elisa suggested.

"The whole week? I can't believe you're doing this for me," Jackie said, visibly touched.

"From now on, I'll do anything for you," Elisa declared, taking Jackie's hands in hers. "Because I love you, and I refuse to spend the best years of our lives solely focused on chasing petty criminals. They don't deserve it."

"I love you so much," Jackie responded, moving closer and kissing her. Her lips were slightly salty from her tears, but it was one of the sweetest kisses they had ever shared.

Part 2

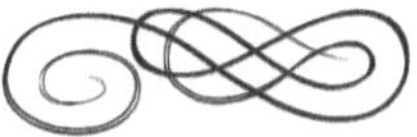

Snow Moon

11

Family Business

"What a good boy!" Jackie extended her hand and patted the soft blue scales of Rei, a dragon three times bigger than an average horse. Rei closed his yellow eyes and purred, delighted by her tenderness. Jackie laughed. "I missed you, too."

They were at the barn entrance, enjoying an unusually warm winter evening. A pink sunset colored the snow around them and made Rei's magnificent scales glow.

"Hey, should I be jealous?" Theo asked as he walked out of the barn, shaking hay from his black coat. One straw got stuck in his flaming hair, and he removed it with a smile.

"Maybe," Jackie teased him. Even after two days here, she still couldn't get used to seeing her old friend, now a professional guardian, in this village-like setting. Since Theo had moved to Triville, he immediately started helping at the farm where Rei lived with his sibling, a red dragon named Rose. Theo even occupied one of the rooms in the huge household that belonged to Kyle Turner, a dragon tamer, as people called him.

Theo neared Rei and moved his hand along the dragon's spine. "Pal, don't get used to this. Ladies make you too soft."

Jackie scratched the dragon's ear. "But he *is* soft! I imagined him hunting all day and setting places on fire. But he is just adorable."

"He actually did set the old barn on fire," Theo said with a soft chuckle. His blue eyes looked up into the sky as he got lost in his memories. "Yes, several weeks after I brought him to this farm. Kyle said he probably missed me badly. So I started visiting him regularly after that."

"And when you graduated from The Academy, you moved here and lived happily ever after," Jackie finished the story that she knew by heart.

"Exactly," Theo confirmed. "And as I'm the only guardian who has a dragon, I often take Rei to different distant places where we investigate tricky crimes."

Jackie gave him a respectful look. With his sharp detective mind, Theo had not only been successfully working in a local Guardian House. He quickly became famous in Lake Kingdom because he could travel basically anywhere. *A rare gem*, as people often called him in newspapers. "Ah, Theo. Sometimes, I wish I could lead this lifestyle – flying everywhere, exploring the wonders of nature."

"Well, I mostly explore the limits of human cruelty," he complained. "But sometimes we really visit wonderful places, like mountain lakes and canyons."

"Wanna make me jealous?" Jackie sighed as she imagined the gorgeous landscapes floating under her feet, a rare view that she might never have a chance to see.

He scratched his chin. "Actually... What do you think about a short trip to the mountains tomorrow? We'll take Rei and Elisa and spend the whole day in the air."

Her lips parted in awe. "I would love that. If Elisa won't mind!"

"Of course, she won't." He chuckled. "She once flew with me, if you remember."

Jackie nodded. It was impossible to forget that moment when they caught the leader of the criminal gang. It was also the eve of the day when she got together with Elisa. "I do remember. It's hard to believe it was three years ago."

"Time flies." Theo checked a time crystal on his wrist and frowned. "By the way, I'm on duty tonight, so I gotta go."

Jackie rose. "Already?!"

"Yes." Theo smiled and shifted his eyes to Rei. "Alright, pal, it's time to get to bed."

The dragon pressed his long ears to his back, lying on the ground and pretending not to hear him.

Jackie couldn't help laughing. "He might want more attention."

"And he'll get all of it tomorrow," Theo patted Rei's back. "C'mon, man. Get up!"

Rei sighed, gave Jackie a sad look, and slowly walked to the barn. Theo 3.25closed the door after him. "Sorry, he's just always like this when his sister is away. It's heartbreaking sometimes. Usually, he is very cheerful."

"It's life." Jackie shrugged. "And I'm glad to help. You know that."

"Of course." Theo gave her a warm look. "Alright, see you tomorrow."

She smiled. "Good luck with your duty!"

Jackie changed her winter boots at the house to comfy slippers decorated with fluffy white pom-poms. She had met Kyle's wife only once, and it was three years ago when Julia saved her life. As Jackie learned, since their arrival in Triville, Julia was absent because she was urgently called to a distant city. With her rare Healing Gift, Julia often traveled with the second dragon, Rose.

Even though Jackie didn't know her closely, she could imagine Julia's character. She only needed to use her detective eye as she admired the small things that made this home so cozy. Jackie stepped into a spacious hall where the furniture was covered with soft white blankets and small pillows with bright red and green patterns. A huge fireplace made of white stones was decorated with candles and antique accessories, reflecting Julia's good taste and love of order. *Maybe she's a perfectionist*, Jackie decided.

What amazed Jackie was that, unlike many families, they didn't bring a New Year tree into the house to decorate it. Instead, they covered the pine in their yard with colorful glass spheres glowing in the sunlight. What a sweet gesture toward preserving nature!

The baking chicken smell reached her nose, and Jackie walked to the kitchen. She stopped at the threshold, admiring Elisa. Tonight, she wore an apron, and with her golden curls banded in a knot, she looked like a caring wife. Elisa was fully focused on cutting the veggies for the salad and didn't notice her. Jackie widened her eyes, trying to remember the last time Elisa attempted to cook something. Nothing came to her mind. *Gee, she really tries hard.*

Kyle, a man with blue eyes and broad shoulders, pulled a tray with chicken from the oven and placed it on the table. He removed his mittens and smiled at Jackie. "How is Rei?"

Jackie shrugged and came to the table. "Better today. Theo says he misses his sister badly."

Kyle's look became dull. "I know. And this is exactly how I miss my wife, who took her and flew away."

"Oh, don't be such a drama queen." Elisa poked him with her elbow. "You have us to interact with you."

"Well, it's not the same." Kyle took a fine red wine and poured it into the crystal glasses. "But I'm glad that you finally made it here."

Jackie raised her glass. "I'm glad to finally meet you. For the friend's reunion!"

Elisa's hands were all covered with veggie juices, so she didn't touch the glass but nodded in response. "For reunion!"

Jackie took a sip and smiled. "So, Kyle. I couldn't help noticing that it was just Rei and a couple of unborn eggs in the barn. Is this business going well?"

Kyle finished his glass in two gulps before replying. "It's complicated."

"Well, as my friend says, life never gets easier." Elisa finished cutting the veggies and added them to the salad bowl. She wiped her hands with the towel. "That's why you have friends. I bet that whatever it is, we can brainstorm it and figure something out."

Jackie nodded. "True. So what's that? You need to steal more eggs?"

"Chill." Elisa giggled. "That was a one-time adventure."

"But Theo is constantly flying to the caves alone. I guess a little help won't hurt."

Kyle waved his hand. "Okay, it's not about the quantity of the dragons. We have the demands, yes, but we get the eggs only when someone orders them. So, we never run out of customers, and we don't even spend much on raising them."

"Then what's the issue?" Elisa wondered.

He took a seat in the chair. "These creatures are worth a lot, and they give a lot of advantages to the people who have them."

"To the ones who can afford them," Elisa added.

"Exactly. But I think it's unfair that our guardians in Triville don't have them."

Jackie nodded. Somehow, no local guardian except Theo had a dragon, and it still was a serious problem when crime happened in a distant small town where people couldn't get professional help fast.

"Because it's expensive to maintain them," Elisa pointed out. "A dragon is a luxury. They need a lot of space, food, and proper care."

Jackie and Kyle exchanged glances in silence. Somehow, all of them understood this, but no one ever raised this question. Except Elisa. This is what Jackie loved about her – she was never afraid to look in the face of new obstacles, whatever it was.

"You are right," Kyle said. "That's why only rich people have them, and we literally built a business on it. But we got a complication I couldn't foresee. I thought that only good people could deserve the respect of a dragon, but I was wrong. People buy dragons here, and we train them, alright. But some of these people sold the eggs of grown-up reptiles to hell knows who. Someone started committing crimes in different cities, and they easily get away with it as they fly faster than the guardians can chase them." Kyle shook his head. "It's all my fault."

Elisa raised her eyebrows. "How is this your fault? What can you do about crimes?"

He sighed. "The King sent us a written warning recently. Apparently, it's easier for them to shut this place down than to work on improving their army."

They went silent. Jackie's heart ached as she imagined Rei being forced back into the wild. Living for so long among humans, he might simply not survive. How quickly everything can be ruined. When the farm just opened, people were so excited about taming these reptiles, and the tourists started visiting Triville to watch the dragons. It brought fame and income to this small town that was actively growing now. "Can they really shut down this place?"

Kyle poured himself another glass. "Their last drop was when they were investigating a very arrogant robbery. The criminals simply took two hundred grand of golden coins and escaped on their dragon."

"I see." Elisa gazed at his glass disapprovingly. She took the plates and started serving the dinner. "It's too late to change anything, so we can try to work on creating a balance. Why can't we create facilities and start teaching the guardians flying?"

"I spoke with Chief Morris about it," Kyle replied. "He says the same thing – it takes too long and is too risky. It usually takes around a year until the dragon can carry the person, so he doesn't consider it a good investment."

Elisa sneered. "And the budget is tight, as he claims."

"It's always something more important they need to pay for." Kyle took one of the plates and stubbed his fork into a chicken leg. "I even agreed to provide the reptiles for free, so the government would only need to take care of food and maintenance. But they rejected my offer."

Jackie chewed her food slowly, thinking. Food always helped her channel her thoughts, especially if it was so delicious. "As a mind-reader, I learned a very interesting thing about people – they always look for the easiest ways. I can tell exactly why they made this decision – it is easier for them to cut this rope rather than build a complicated structure. In this case, they could avoid all the hassle, like building special facilities – barns, training centers, and farms to provide food to the dragons. Plus, they wouldn't have to hire grooms, veterinarians, and who knows what else –"

"Fair enough." Kyle gave her a murky look. "But this observation doesn't help."

"Sorry," Jackie said in a soft voice. "I just want you to realize how much is at stake before I tell you what to do. You might not agree to do it before you know the real cost of things."

Kyle poured more wine into her glass. "Go on."

Jackie twisted the glass in her hand as the candlelight played in the ruby liquid. "From now on, Theo should carefully check every request for help that he accepts from distant towns. If you prove that the crime could threaten the safety of the Kingdom, and you prevented it only because you have the dragon, a Guardian Chief will listen. And then, we will make a petition and send it to the King."

"You think the King will listen?"

Jackie shook her head. "Of course not. You will need to do another thing – you must scare him to death by providing some information."

"Which information?"

"The King is a strong, powerful man, and the worst nightmare of a powerful person is to lose control." Jackie put her glass on a table and leaned closer, lowering her voice. "You must make them think that even people with average income can massively raise dragons without their or your control."

Kyle gave her a puzzled look. "But I personally teach them. And they cannot really train anyone because every dragon is unique. Maybe the King is right, and if they totally forbid them –"

"They won't," Jackie interrupted him. "Because you'll tell your secret of raising them to everyone."

He widened his eyes. "How?"

Elisa's eyes sparkled. "I know what she means! We were working on a story publishing, and the idea was to share Jackie's story to help change people's attitudes towards women. You can issue a manual describing all known breeds and their special traits. If you release it –"

"The government will lose control over this situation," Kyle said. "But we will lose it too, then."

"Yes," Jackie agreed. "And again, I will ask – how much are you ready to sacrifice to make your idea live?"

Elisa put her hand on Kyle's shoulder and looked into his eyes. "Whatever you decide, we're always by your side."

He shifted his eyes across the room. "Erm... that advice was priceless. Really. It might work just fine."

"See, a piece of cake!" Elisa winked and bit into a loaf of baked potato.

"The only problem is that I'm not a writer. I haven't held a pen since high school."

"I would be glad to help you with writing," Jackie suggested. "Just to have a place to start."

"She really can," Elisa confirmed. "That book she wrote... It's brilliant."

Jackie blushed. "Ah, don't exaggerate... It's our story. That's why you think so."

Kyle laughed. "It truly deserves to be published."

Jackie's fork stopped on the way to her mouth. Her cheeks flushed. "What?! Don't tell me you read it."

"Theo showed me a blueprint that you brought with you. It's really good."

"See?!" Elisa smiled. Her gaze stopped at Jackie, and she mustered a puppy look. "Sorry, dear. I tried to brainstorm if we can find another agent soon."

Jackie placed the food in her mouth, chewing. Maybe it wasn't nice of Elisa to do it without asking, but on the other hand, the story would be available for reading. It just was weird to realize that it might be read by people who knew her personally. What would her mom say? Ok, mom is mom. But what about dad? She shook her head, trying to focus on dinner and not on her worries. It was better to change the subject. "So you guys were friends in school?"

Elisa and Kyle exchanged glances.

"It's a very complicated story," Elisa said.

Jackie rested her head on her palm. "I would love to hear it, then."

12

A Cult

At midnight, Elisa stopped in the front yard of The Guardian House. The two-story building, constructed of black stones, loomed over her like a giant shadow. The rooftop, adorned with a metal dragon, glistened in the moonlight. The stars twinkled in the cold sky above, a reminder of the souls that had departed this world prematurely. First, her mother, then all the high school girls who had broken a few rules and were later murdered.

Elisa had entered this building multiple times as both a victim and a witness, but now she was here for the first time as a guardian. It had been a challenging journey, but she was prepared to see it through to the end. She checked her wicker basket, ensuring that the leftovers from dinner were securely covered with a kitchen towel to keep them warm. Then, she entered the building.

Triville was incredibly small, eliminating the need for an observation tower. Instead, the guardians utilized a special room on the top floor, featuring two large windows on opposite walls. These windows now offered a breathtaking view of the slumbering winter town, bathed in a blue glow emanating from the tree trunks.

"Hey, Sparkle!" Theo greeted as Elisa entered. The room was dimly lit, with only a couple of candles on his desk illuminating his cheerful face.

"Hey," Elisa replied with a smile, placing the basket of food on his desk. The aroma of baked chicken and potatoes wafted through the room.

Theo, unable to contain his hunger, eagerly grabbed a fork, its metal surface gleaming in the candlelight. "Oh, thanks for bringing this!"

Elisa settled into a chair and observed as Theo devoured his meal. "No problem. By the way, Jackie is currently busy assisting Kyle with his writing."

"Huh?" Theo gave her a puzzled look while still chewing.

She chuckled at Theo's hearty appetite, a trait she remembered from their days as cadets that had remained unchanged. Elisa handed him a paper napkin and elaborated, "He's working on a little project. Despite the setback with her agent, Jackie is eager to assist someone in bringing their book to life. Isn't it adorable?"

Theo finished his meal and wiped his lips. "It is. And you two make a great couple."

Elisa smiled, flattered. "Supporting someone you love isn't too difficult."

"I admire that mindset," Theo remarked, giving her a knowing look. "You know, I'm currently investigating a particularly sensitive case, and I wouldn't mind hearing your professional opinion. If you have the time, of course."

"I'm all ears."

Theo rose from his seat to retrieve a folder from one of the shelves. Taking advantage of the moment, Elisa cleared the dishes from the desk and readied herself to delve back into detective work. The allure of a new investigation always held her in its grip, commanding her full attention. Somewhere in the recesses of her mind, she recalled her promise to Jackie to concentrate on their vacation. However, with Jackie preoccupied as well, a brief brainstorming session wouldn't hurt.

Theo placed an open folder in front of her, and Elisa picked up the first page of the report, beginning to read.

A Murder Case #1124-10-724
 Victim's Name: Angela Gladdys
Age: Eighteen years old
Approximate Time of Death: November 8th
Cause of Death: Fireball wound to the chest
Details from the Crime Scene:
- Physical Traces: Multiple small boot prints. Note: Sole print analysis indicates these boots are designed for females.
- Magic Traces: Numerous energy patterns detected. Note: None of the energy patterns matched any in the database.

Theodore Thomas, a senior detective at Trillville Guardian House, authored the report.

Elisa set the report aside. Two other reports involving young women were documented on September 10th and October 9th. Strangely, all three murders occurred within the first third of the month, suggesting a potential pattern. This was a troubling sign. She looked up at Theo. "Where did you say you found them?"

"All the bodies were discovered in the front yards of their respective parents' homes, which facilitated their identification. However, we are at a loss as to the identity of the perpetrator and their motive."

"It must be someone seriously sick," Elisa remarked, her expression darkening. Typically, murderers either left their victims at the scene of the crime or attempted to conceal the bodies in remote locations. The act of leaving the bodies at the victims' family homes was unprecedented in her experience. However, it also provided a crucial clue – the killer possessed intimate knowledge of the victims' identities and residences.

Theo shuffled through the pages and presented three sketches of the victims. "They hailed from different small towns and villages, making it unlikely that they had crossed paths. The common thread among them is that their families were all religious."

Elisa studied the images of the three women, each adorned in white nightgowns embellished with a small sun pattern along the collar lines and sleeves. "Why are they dressed alike?"

"It's another peculiar aspect," Theo acknowledged. "According to their families, the women departed after disputes regarding their disobedience and failure to adhere to community regulations. None of them took extra clothing with them."

"Interesting," Elisa mused, arranging the pictures before her as she sought additional clues. "So, they must have acquired the nightgowns from the same location. But where?"

"I initially suspected that these young women may have stopped at the same motel that provided the nightgowns. However, after checking all nearby motels, I found no matches."

Elisa pondered this information, her lip caught between her teeth as she contemplated the situation.

"The most concerning aspect is that the murders occur at intervals of approximately 29-30 days, allowing me to predict when the next one might take place. Yet, I have no insight into the location or the next victim."

Elisa blinked in realization. "29-30 days... like a moon cycle."

"Yes, they were all killed on a full moon," Theo confirmed.

Elisa turned to the window, gazing at the night sky where the almost full moon cast its glow among the twinkling stars. "How much time do we have to stop the next murder?"

"Too little. The next projected crime date is December 8th, which is tomorrow night," Theo replied, running a hand through his red hair. "Honestly, I'm at a loss on where to begin the search."

"What about your gut instinct?" Elisa inquired. She recalled their teacher, Don, advising them to trust their intuition in moments of uncertainty. While it often proved unreliable, it was better than having no direction at all.

Theo shrugged. "I considered taking Rei and flying over the mountains, attempting to spot any signs of fire or unusual activity. But it seems impractical."

"Why not? It's clearly some kind of cult. Typically, cults gather in isolated areas not too far from town. They likely conduct their rituals, then return the victim home before moving on to the next location."

"Consider this – the victims were found dressed only in night-gowns, indicating they were not outdoors, especially in this cold weather. Locating the specific building where the ritual takes place would be akin to finding a needle in a haystack."

Elisa nodded in understanding. "It may be challenging to prevent the next crime, but we can still try to anticipate where they might leave the body of the next victim."

Theo interlocked his fingers, expressing his concern. "The other major issue is that the search area is vast, and I'm the only one..."

"Hold on," Elisa interrupted him, a plan forming in her mind. She picked up a candle and motioned for Theo to follow her.

They arrived at a map hanging on the wall, the candle's flickering light casting dancing shadows across its surface.

"Where was the first body discovered?" Elisa inquired.

"That's not where they were killed, remember?"

Giving him a sharp look, Elisa urged him to indicate the location on the map. He pointed to a village nestled in the mountains near Santos.

"Alright. Where was the second one found?"

"Here," Theo shifted his hand to the right, indicating a location closer to the mountains that separated Triville from the Cursed Plateau, an area known for its strong cold winds. "And the next one was closer to Crystal Caves."

Elisa regarded him with interest. "Theo, you just pointed to places near the same road. Read the road's name."

Turning back to the map, Theo retraced his finger through the locations he had indicated. There was a road passing through all these places, labeled as *Divina Via*. "You think they're traveling along this road?"

"Translated from the ancient language, it means 'Divine Path'," Elisa whispered, leaning in closer to Theo. "Symbolic, isn't it? If I were organizing a cult, I'd stick to this road. I'd stop in small towns and villages to recruit new, unsuspecting young women into my group, only to sacrifice them later on a full moon."

"Incredible!" Theo exclaimed, turning to her with a gleam in his eyes. "Gee, Sparkle. I never realized how much I missed you until now."

"Glad to be of assistance." Elisa chuckled. "I hope this plan works out and you're able to apprehend them."

"Yeah." Theo scratched his chin thoughtfully. "Preventing the next crime will be a challenge."

Elisa shrugged. "As usual. We must do our best."

"We definitely will!" Theo's voice brimmed with excitement. "We'll need to investigate further locations along this road starting tomorrow morning. We should check for reports of missing girls at local Guardian Houses. If we set out by noon, we'll have ample time to reach the Crystal Caves and conduct our research."

"Wait a moment," Elisa said, taking a step back. "While I was happy to assist you in finding a lead, you know that I made a promise to Jackie –"

"Relax, I've already taken care of it," Theo reassured her, waving his hand dismissively. "I spoke to Jackie before coming here, and she's on board for a little field trip. I don't think she'll mind if tomorrow I ask her to make a few stops to investigate something suspicious related to a murder case."

Elisa paused, adjusting to the idea of diving into a new investigation and reuniting with a team that had become more than just colleagues. She smiled and embraced him tightly. "I missed you too."

13

An Interview

Jackie sat in a plush chair, a brand-new notebook on her lap. The flames flickered in the fireplace, casting dancing gleams on the soft yellow pages. It was always a bit daunting to start a new chapter, no matter how much she practiced. So many thoughts swirled in her head, causing her to doubt if it was worth it. To quiet them, all she needed to do was to start writing.

"So, what are we going to do?" Kyle asked. He sat on a sofa in front of her, cradling a cup of steaming tea. Jackie had made him drink it to counteract the effects of the wine he had consumed during dinner. Now, Kyle appeared relaxed yet focused – a perfect combination.

"Let's begin with the introduction," she suggested, twirling a pencil in her hand. "Then you can take it from there. Just describe the dragon breeds and everything important you have learned about them."

He nodded. "Of course. I have learned a great deal over the years."

"So, how did you come up with the idea to start a dragon farm?"

He smiled, lost in his memories. "It all started because of a girl."

She paused, intrigued. "A girl?"

"Yes. Julia is the most amazing person I've ever met – tender, kind, beautiful... I fell deeply in love with her in high school. Then she discovered her unique Gift, and she was thrilled to begin helping others. She dreamed of traveling across the Kingdom, saving lives. She believed she was destined for this role and that Divine power would shield her from any evil individuals who might try to exploit her precious Gift for their own gain. But I was not as certain. All I could think about was how to protect her."

Jackie quickly jotted down her notes as he spoke. "You could become her protector and travel together. Why dragons?"

He shrugged. "I once came across a legend about them, and it seemed so romantic to have such an amazing and loyal creature. To be able to rely on it completely, knowing that the dragon would always keep her safe wherever she went. People fear them, and if she were to stop in the middle of a forest, no wild animal would dare to cross paths with a dragon. No one wants to become their dinner."

"Everything eventually unfolded as you had envisioned," Jackie observed. Julia, now his wife, was currently away but expected to return at any moment.

He nodded. "It was just a dream initially. When the idea came to me, I shared it with Elisa. Who would have thought that you guys would actually procure the dragon eggs for me?"

Jackie chuckled. Stealing from the dragons had been an unforgettable adventure and the first time their group had come together, overcoming grave danger. At that time, she had no inkling of where that journey would ultimately lead them.

"Yes, now she is with Rose, her dragon," Kyle said, his voice tinged with sadness. He turned towards the darkened window, his eyes glistening with unshed tears.

"You must miss her terribly," Jackie surmised.

He took a deep breath and blinked, attempting to dispel the melancholy that lingered. However, his efforts proved futile. "I do, but it's more than that. It's unsettling to realize that no matter what I do, I can't shield her from every danger."

Jackie set her pencil down. It was evident that Kyle harbored a troubling secret, one that influenced his behavior. This revelation shed light on his hesitance in safeguarding his family's business. *Is there an unresolved conflict between Kyle and Julia?* If so, it could pose a significant obstacle to writing the book and maintaining the dragon farm. *Can I help them somehow?*

Knowing that men often struggled to express their personal feelings, Jackie hesitated to use her Gift to delve into Kyle's thoughts. It would be too intrusive. Instead, she decided to take a different approach. Perhaps by sharing her own vulnerabilities, she could establish a foundation of trust. "That's true. Even with our magic, we aren't completely shielded. When I first entered The Academy, I felt like my life was over. Following the assault, I was engulfed in darkness for months. However, with the support of my friends, I eventually managed to overcome it."

"I do everything in my power to support her," Kyle said, his voice quivering. "But it never feels like enough. Since that... tragic incident, she has been acting as though nothing happened. Yet, every time I gaze into her eyes, I see a profound emptiness. If only I knew how to help her."

Jackie set her notebook aside. She was unaware of the specifics of Julia's situation, but that was inconsequential. Whatever had transpired, she was determined to utilize her skills to aid this family. "Opening up can be challenging, especially to those we hold dear. We fear that our problems may burden them, even at our lowest points. However, by bottling up our emotions, we only deepen our wounds."

"Is there no way out of this?"

"I can speak with her," Jackie proposed. "I have experience working with women who have endured domestic violence, child loss, and other life-altering tragedies. I have witnessed how a glimmer of hope can ignite in their eyes, even after enduring the darkest of circumstances. While I cannot guarantee a miraculous solution, I will do everything in my power to help your wife understand that she is not alone in this."

"If she is willing." Kyle sighed, his hands fidgeting with the teacup. "She shuts herself off and refuses to listen."

Jackie's gaze shifted to the notebook resting on the chair handle. "You should consider writing her a letter."

"A letter?" He raised his eyebrows in surprise.

"Yes, a heartfelt letter can help you bypass her emotional barriers," Jackie explained, picking up her pencil and gesturing towards him. "It's a simple yet effective method. Just express to her what you shared with me about your desire to protect her, and it could be the first step towards her healing."

He gazed up at the ceiling. "What an irony! A Healer in need of healing."

"Believe me, those who dedicate themselves to helping others often require healing themselves. I believe that the challenges we face are meant to strengthen our resilience."

"That's an interesting perspective," he agreed. "I used to write poetry and keep a diary. Although it's been a while, I think I can give it a try."

"Great!" Jackie said, clapping her hands together as she stood up. "If you can convince her to take a month off work, I can introduce her to our support group in Middle Lake. We have a strong network of women who can provide assistance."

He stood up. "Thank you, Jackie. For everything."

"That's what friends are for, right?" She handed him the notebook she had used for the interview. "Feel free to refer to the notes if needed. Focus on resolving this first. The rest of your book will fall into place once you do."

"Gosh, I almost forgot about the book," he muttered, rubbing his forehead. "And the plan to save the farm. It all seems insignificant now."

"That's true. Nothing else matters if we are broken inside. Just give it time."

He nodded and let out a yawn. "I hope Elisa returns soon."

"Unless she's caught up in a new murder case," Jackie quipped.

Kyle chuckled. "You know her too well."

Kyle headed upstairs to work on his letter, leaving Jackie alone. She peered out the window, attempting to discern Elisa's silhouette amidst the glowing blue trees. The nearly full moon cast a heavy weight on her heart. She knew from experience, both as a guardian and a lawyer, that something ominous often occurred during this time of the month.

Is Elisa safe? That's what Jackie often asked herself as she found herself gazing out into the night street. The role of a guardian was perilous, a fact she was well aware of, having once aspired to pursue that path. Despite her apprehension, Jackie refrained from questioning Elisa's work. After all, it was her true calling.

At times, Jackie found herself waiting for Elisa until the break of dawn. She often drifted off to sleep while perched on their spacious windowsill. She had lost count of how frequently she found herself gazing out of that window. Deep down, all she yearned for was to fall asleep in Elisa's arms; that was all that truly mattered to her.

"Do criminals ever take a break?" Jackie inquired, addressing the moon.

"I wish they did, my dear," Elisa's voice responded from behind her.

Startled, Jackie turned to find Elisa standing there. "How did you get in? I was watching the yard."

"I used the kitchen door," Elisa replied, enveloping Jackie in a hug, her hands still chilled from being outside. "It's touching that you wait for me, but you don't have to."

Jackie smiled. "I know. But I'm grateful I lingered a while longer."

Elisa cast a guilty glance at her. "Aren't you going to inquire about my meeting with Theo?"

"I would, but I'd rather not discuss work," Jackie said, planting a kiss on Elisa's cheek. "Not at this moment."

"Fair enough," Elisa agreed, smiling as she took Jackie's hand. "Let's explore a different side of this night."

14

Divine Path

The sun was lowering to the west rim of the horizon, coloring the mountaintops in a gentle pink hue. Rose, the dragon, soared through the skies with her red wings spread wide. Jackie held Elisa tightly as the wind whistled in their ears. Inhaling the fresh air, they both admired the beauty of the landscape below.

Nearby, the Crystal Caves stood, with a small village nestled among them. The neat roofs of the village houses emitted smoke from the chimneys, visible against the backdrop of the empty snow-covered streets.

Elisa raised her hand and shouted, "Let's land here. Inform Theo."

Following her command, Jackie touched the Calling crystal attached to her ear with a copper wire. "Theo, hello?!"

"Yes?" Theo's voice came through, slightly muffled by the wind.

Jackie smiled, grateful for the usefulness of the new device invented by Edward. They had decided to test the technology before introducing it to the authorities, but Jackie was confident that soon, people would not be able to imagine their lives without these magical crystals.

"Jackie, are you there?" Theo's voice came through again.

"Yes!" She shouted, trying to be heard over the wind. "We are landing. You go first."

"Got it," Theo replied.

Rose circled, descending close to the village but not yet touching down. Theo approached from the north, riding a magnificent blue reptile named Rei. Jackie held her breath as she watched him land gracefully on the ground.

It was a delight to travel with Rei's sister, Rose, who was almost twice his size due to their mixed breed. Despite being smaller, Rei always led the way, and Rose obediently followed. Theo chose to ride Rei so that Jackie and Elisa could follow them in the air.

After Rei landed, Rose carefully stepped into the traces left by her older brother.

As they approached the rocks, Rose came to a stop, and Elisa leaped off the dragon onto the ground. She extended a hand to help Jackie climb down. Although not as graceful as Elisa, Jackie managed to navigate the snow without falling.

Theo joined them, rubbing his frozen hands. "How was the flight?"

"I loved it," Jackie replied with a wide smile. "If I could, I would fly all day long."

Theo chuckled. "We should make it a tradition, then."

"I hope we will," Elisa agreed. "But let's focus on cracking this case first."

Theo gazed down at the village below. "Alright, let's head there and ask around."

Jackie nodded, and they began their descent down the mountain trail. This was the third village along the road known as Divine Path, and their mission was to investigate key locations where the cult leaders might be present. Despite their previous unsuccessful attempts, she remained hopeful that the third time would be the charm.

Jackie rapped on the heavy church door. While Elisa headed to the local Guardian House and Theo scoured the local pubs for potential suspects, Jackie's task was to visit the church and alert the priest to report any suspicious cult members to the guardians.

The door creaked open slowly, revealing the face of a man with a neatly trimmed gray beard. Clad in the traditional attire of a priest, he wore a long white robe adorned with golden stripes on the collar and sleeves.

"Can I be of assistance, my daughter?" he inquired in a calm and polite tone.

"That is my hope, Saint Father," Jackie replied, placing her hand on her chest and offering a respectful smile. "I'm here with my guardian companions who are working to prevent a series of heinous crimes. I only require a few minutes of your time."

His once lively blue eyes now held a tinge of sadness. "Crime is a violation of human life, and I'm willing to assist you, no matter how long it may take."

He stepped back to usher her inside, and Jackie entered the church. The interior was illuminated by the warm glow of hundreds of candles lining the walls. Despite the darkness outside, the church seemed to radiate with a brightness akin to daylight. The narrow windows adorned with colorful stained glass mosaics sparkled like precious jewels.

Jackie's mouth fell slightly open as she gazed at the portraits of Saints representing the six core foundations of life: safety, health, love, family, dignity, and truthfulness. She tried to recall the last time she had been in a church, realizing it must have been in her life before The Academy – a life filled with fears that she had ruthlessly buried.

"Isn't it beautiful?" the priest remarked, standing nearby and soaking in the serene atmosphere. "Today, we celebrate the full moon and pay homage to the delicate beauty of human life."

The mention of the full moon refocused Jackie on her mission. "It truly is amazing, Saint Father. I hope it will help us save a life today."

"You must have traveled a long road, daughter. Before I inquire further, may I offer you a hot drink?" The priest's compassionate gaze met hers as he gestured towards his chamber. Jackie followed him inside.

The priest's office was small and inviting. After settling into a plush chair, she enjoyed a cup of fragrant raspberry tea.

"So, what brings you here?" He inquired as he took his seat behind the desk. In this setting, he appeared more approachable, someone Jackie could speak openly with.

Taking a sip of the delicious tea, Jackie placed the cup on her lap. "Saint Father, I'm here because three young women have been murdered in the past three months, each crime occurring during a full moon."

Pain flickered in his eyes, and he blinked it away. "How dreadful! Would you like me to pray with you to seek guidance on how to stop it?"

Jackie sighed. "I'm afraid a prayer won't suffice this time. My guardian friend has discovered that all the women were killed by a religious cult."

The Saint Father shook his head in disbelief. "Evil often manifests in the most unexpected forms. Murder should never be associated with any religion." He gestured for her to continue.

"All we have gathered is that a stranger recruits innocent women into their twisted beliefs, ultimately sacrificing their lives using fireball spells."

The priest fell silent, his gaze fixed on the bookshelf. "Fireballs? Oh, no... wait, do they target the girls who attempt to flee?"

"Yes," Jackie confirmed. "How did you know that? Have you encountered any of them?"

Instead of responding, the priest stood up and walked over to the bookshelf. Within seconds, he retrieved a black book and flipped it open to a page in the middle, engrossed in reading. Jackie fidgeted, tapping her fingers on the chair handle, eager to learn more about the cult but hesitant to interrupt him.

"Here," he said, approaching Jackie and placing a book in front of her. She gazed at the image of a woman, appearing to be in her early forties based on the light wrinkles around her blue eyes.

"Who is she?" Jackie inquired in a hushed tone.

The Saint Father let out a deep sigh and clasped his hands together. "Claudia. She was one of the most dedicated women who led the Divine community in Triville. I knew her through the church's leaders and senior members, as we held quarterly meetings to share spiritual experiences and support one another through challenges. One day, she approached me, clearly burdened with profound sorrow.

"Claudia's daughter possessed a forbidden fire Gift and had been placed in Mercy House. However, the girl managed to escape and return home. Claudia believed she had to allow a Gift Hunter to kill her daughter to prevent future disobedience, specifying that she must be killed with a fireball."

"Wouldn't the girl be immune to fireball attacks with her Gift of fire?" Jackie inquired.

"By that time, her powers had been stripped from her. This was the practice in Mercy Houses – they would remove all magical abilities," the priest explained, his voice faltering as he took a seat. "I advised Claudia to protect her daughter at all costs, but she hesitated to intervene. The tragedy weighed heavily on her. After her daughter's death, Claudia asked me to release her from her sorrows. Naturally, I refused. I gave her time to distance herself from the community, and she disappeared from our midst."

"And all of this took place in Triville?"

"Yes, everything unfolded in Triville. Claudia's fixation on the fireball concept may have played a role in all of this. You can use this portrait to track her whereabouts. With her knack for organization and persuasion, she could very well be connected to the cult you are investigating."

Jackie nodded, still reeling from the revelations. While she was certain Elisa was aware of this tale, the gravity of the situation hit her hard. She gazed at the priest with a sorrowful expression. "Why did you exile her?"

"Because, as I mentioned, murder is never a viable solution. During that era, it was forbidden for women to possess destructive magic. Those seeking control propagated fear, claiming that if women wielded powers traditionally held by men, it would disrupt the balance of magic and usher in chaos. Consequently, young women were either stripped of their abilities or eliminated. Such actions were deemed unacceptable, as the sanctity of human life should always take precedence."

"What is a woman to do when torn between human laws and Divine truths?" Jackie pondered aloud.

The priest offered her a compassionate gaze. "Divine truth is boundless and rooted in eternal love. Human truth, on the other hand, is finite and shaped by individual regulations. While the decision may appear clear to me, my dear daughter, it is not a simple one. We reside among humans, and safeguarding Divine truth can often put our lives in danger."

"That can indeed be a challenging reality. I wish it were different."

"One day, it will be," the priest reassured her with a warm smile. "However, the journey is not an easy one, for this world is fraught with fears and shadows. Remember, Jackie, that you carry your Light within you. Trusting in its guidance will lead you down the right path, no matter how arduous it may seem."

Her heart warmed at his comforting words, silently agreeing with his wisdom. Jackie finished her tea, realizing it was time to depart and allow the priest to continue his duties. She rose from her seat. "Thank you, Saint Father. It's been an honor to meet you and receive your assistance and counsel."

He also stood up. "I'll keep you and your mission in my prayers, daughter."

15

The Drop

At eight in the evening, Jackie walked into the tavern near the central square. Elisa was already there, shivering from the cold and tightening her black woolen scarf around her upper body.

"Gee, it's so cold!" Elisa complained. "You know how much I hate these stupid criminals, but more than anything, I hate when they make me freeze!"

Jackie took a seat and gave her a calm look. "We both know no cold can stop you from doing this job."

Elisa chuckled. "True. But sometimes I wish it could be a bit more comfortable."

The waitress brought two plates of hot soup, and they picked up their spoons. After a long day of chasing criminals, the food seemed twice as tasty.

"I had a really good visit to the church," Jackie smiled as she finished her soup, feeling it pleasantly settle in her stomach.

Elisa gave her a perplexed look. "Hey, we agreed not to share our search results unless we're all back together."

"It's not about our search." Jackie waved her hand, explaining. "What I mean is that it was so... peaceful."

Elisa snickered. "Oh, so this time they didn't suggest praying for our success for 'a reasonable price'?"

"No. This visit was special. It made me look at everything differently." She pointed at the dark window. "What do you see outside?"

"Huh... A snowy street?" Elisa suggested.

"Exactly. But if you add a bit of hope and imagination, you will see the future of our Kingdom. On these streets, I see people strolling and chatting, happy with their calm lives. I also see the guardians flying above on their dragons."

"And they communicate using these wonderful crystals," Elisa added, touching her ear where her crystal rested.

"No doubt." Jackie's eyes shifted up to the ceiling. "What if this is a historical moment? What if it's *us* who create a new version of future reality? I think we'll manage to find the right way to save the dragon farm. We just need to believe in it and act accordingly."

Elisa took her hands in hers. "With you, I can believe in everything."

The doors opened, and Theo walked into the tavern. His face was murky. He staggered to their table and fell into the chair. "I didn't find anything worthy but the rumors about the woman who escaped home after murdering her husband."

"It's not quite a rumor," Elisa said. "I was in a Guardian House and found out there was a fire in the town at the end of October. After that, a young woman argued with her husband and accidentally pushed him. Unfortunately, he died in the hospital. They refused to arrest her, and she went to Middle Lake, where her trace was lost. I can send a letter to them just to make sure she is fine, and they didn't overlook her."

"Whoa, Sparkle." Theo gasped. "Next time, I'll be visiting a Guardian House. These pubs are exhausting and mostly a waste of time."

"What was her name?" Jackie asked in a trembling voice. In November, when she was working in a remand center, she met a young woman with the same story. She couldn't believe it was a coincidence.

Elisa narrowed her eyes, trying to recall. "Casey... or Carry..."

Jackie's heart skipped a beat. "Carry Wilson?!"

"Yes." Elisa gave her a surprised look. "What the heck? Did you find something about her?"

"She was my client. And before we left for vacation, I visited her. Carry looked so cheerful and said she finally found her purpose."

"A purpose?"

Jackie nodded in silence. Now Carry's behavior could be explained. She never healed from her trauma. In fact, someone manipulated her, supplying her vulnerable mind with false hopes.

"Well, if she became a victim of this cult, we can't do much to save her life," Theo said with regret in his voice. "It's too late. But we can watch her parents' home tonight and see if her murderers show up to drop... You know." He didn't dare to pronounce the words 'her dead body,' and Jackie appreciated it.

She made herself look at him. "I can't believe they made the long road to Middle Lake and back just for the sake of this sacrifice."

"Why not?" Elisa asked. "It makes sense. I bet this cult is located near overcrowded Middle Lake, so they can easily find new victims. This shithole is full of people in despair. The cult members simply look for someone with parents living near the Divine path, then make a kill and drop the body."

Jackie stared at her without blinking. Sometimes, her directness stung like a sharp needle.

Theo poked Elisa's shoulder. "Easy, she is still in shock! After all, Jackie knew the victim personally."

Elisa gave her an apologetic look. "Sorry, my dear. But as guardians, we operate with theories. I hope we're wrong, and it's not your Carry, but still, we need to check it."

"I understand. I just hope we'll catch these criminals tonight."

"We won't," Theo said.

They gave him a puzzled look.

The waitress brought his order, and Theo waved his spoon in the air, explaining. "A cult, like any gang, has its hierarchy. Probably, they make younger cult members do the drop, and in case this small fish gets caught, the organizers disappear. It would be more effective to follow the person who will lead us to where all the members gather. Thus, we'll catch all of them."

"It's a good idea," Elisa agreed.

"It is," Jackie admitted. When they were cadets, Walter's team tried to catch the criminal gang multiple times before getting to their leader.

Theo finished his food within two minutes and glanced at his time crystal. "Then let's go. We need to find out where the house is and take our positions. I guess I'll be nearby with Rose and Rei, so after it's done, we'll chase the criminals and figure out where they stopped for the night."

"We have to be there, watching this crime?" Jackie asked in a tragic whisper.

"Exactly," Elisa confirmed. "We'll keep silent, so they never realize they are being watched."

Close to midnight, they were sitting in the gazebo that faced the front yard of a big house. The windows were dark, indicating that all the household members were asleep. Little did they know what awaited them.

Jackie rubbed her frozen hands. "If the cult members kill their victims at night when the moon rises, they must be nearby to deliver a body, which means that Carry could still be alive. Are you sure we can't do anything to stop them?"

"Oh, dear..." Elisa gave her a remorseful look. "I wish we could save Carry. If you had any of her belongings, we could perform a Searching spell to find her. But you don't."

Jackie hugged herself to stop shivering. Everything Elisa said made perfect sense. But it didn't make her feel any better. "Why didn't I bring something with me? Like a hairpin?"

"Well, first, you had no idea about this cult before we arrived in Triville. Neither did I. And secondly... did she ever give you any personal belongings?"

Jackie shook her head.

"Then it's not your fault it happened this way." Elisa stood up and leaned on the wooden railings. "Let's hope her sacrifice will help us stop this chain of crimes."

Jackie took a deep sigh and faced the moon. Now, it was full, like a perfectly-shaped round face that watched them in silence, selfishly staying aside from all human tragedies.

The puffing of a horse made her turn back. Someone was riding by the street, a lantern illuminating a wooden cart and a horseman. The horseman wore a black cloak with a wide hood covering the whole face, so it wasn't possible to say if it was a man or a woman.

Without speaking, Elisa and Jackie kneeled on the floor. The horseman stopped near the pavement leading to the house and dismounted the horse. Jackie held her breath, her heart making painful beats in her chest. Suddenly, she forgot about the cold. Instead, sweat rolled down her spine.

The horseman neared the porch, carrying something heavy and wrapped in a dark cloth. He placed his load near the stairs, kneeled on the ground, and drew a five-beam star in the air, whispering something. *A spell?*

Jackie turned to Elisa, a numb question frozen in her eyes.

"Wait here," Elisa whispered. Then, she quietly crawled from the gazebo and ran to the street. Her steps were almost silent in the fresh snow powder covering the ground.

Jackie turned back to the mysterious cult member, trying to guess who it might be based on the silhouette. The lantern was on the ground, making visible only thin white hands that were moving over the dark cloak, unwrapping the dead body. *The suspect is a woman, then.*

Jackie lowered her eyes to the victim. Now, she could clearly see the nightgown and familiar pale face with closed eyes. *Carry.* To stifle a scream, Jackie bit her lip hard. A taste of blood filled her mouth, but she didn't feel any physical pain.

A piece of cloth tied around Carry got stuck, and her murderer leaned closer to remove it. Her hood fell off, and her pale face shone in the moonlight. She was in her mid-forties, her eyes surrounded by light wrinkles. Jackie opened her eyes widely as she recognized the suspect woman, Claudia. Saint Father had shown her this woman's portrait in the church several hours ago. Jackie swallowed. *Where the heck is Elisa?*

The horse neighed in the street, and the woman rushed to her cart, not forgetting to put her hood on.

Elisa appeared nearby in just a few seconds. "Ready. I stole a bracelet from the roadbag, and I bet it belongs to the suspect. So now we can use a Searching spell to chase her."

"Perfect." Jackie nodded and attached her Calling crystal to her ear. "I'll tell Theo to be ready."

In the street, they rushed in the park's direction. At the gates, they stopped to catch their breath. Theo was standing in the glade, his hands up. As Jackie learned, this is how he called the dragons. They formed a special bond, and he could ask Rei to get to him using his mental energy. Rose simply followed him as they were together today. Before they had taken their positions to catch a cult member, Theo reasoned that bringing the dragons too close would ruin the thing as the criminal's horse might sense them and get scared. Now, after the suspect was about to leave the town, they could start the chase.

The dragons appeared in the dark skies, piercing the light clouds. Before they landed, Jackie pulled Elisa's sleeve. "I need to tell you something important."

Elisa's eyebrows knitted. "Can it wait? We need to rush as the Searching spell has a distance limit."

"I know. But it's about that suspect woman. I recognized her from the picture I saw in the church today. She used to be a leader of one Divine community."

"Well, it would explain her obsession."

Jackie looked at her without blinking. Her lower lip still throbbed after she bit it so hard. "That community was in Triville, so you might know her. Her daughter was murdered after she escaped Mercy House. Her name is –"

"Claudia," Elisa said.

Jackie nodded. "So you do know her."

Theo came closer. "If I heard correctly, you used to know the cult member?"

Elisa touched her flushing cheeks. "At that time, she wasn't like that. I called her Auntie Claudia and played in her backyard with her son."

"She has a son?!" They asked together.

Elisa nodded. "Her full name is Claudia Turner. And unfortunately, she is Kyle's mother."

A heavy silence hung in the park, and the dragons quietly landed nearby. Rei came closer and placed his head on Theo's shoulder, intrigued by their conversation.

Theo patted him. "Get ready, buddy. We are about to arrest the mother of your uncle Kyle."

Rei gave him a look full of compassion. Rose stepped nearby and extended one of her wings, letting Jackie and Elisa mount her.

16

A Silver Star

The bright winter sun shone through the half-closed curtains, tickling Jackie's eyelashes. She blinked and sat up, slowly acknowledging where she was. During their stay at Triville, she and Elisa were placed in this small, cozy bedroom. It was the fourth day of their vacation, but still, Jackie couldn't get used to waking up in someone else's house. Elisa was sleeping nearby, her golden locks spread over the snow-white pillow. Jackie moved the blanket up to cover her bare shoulders, and Elisa smiled in her dream.

Jackie put on her clothes and walked downstairs. The smells of cinnamon and chocolate baking filled the living room, making her walk faster. In the kitchen, she stopped, watching Julia, the mistress of the house. Today, Julia wore a white-trimmed apron on top of her spotless blue dress. Holding a spatula, she was fully focused on placing cookies from the hot tray into the crystal dish. The jug of fresh milk rested on the kitchen table.

"Good morning!" Jackie smiled, happy to finally have a chance to get to know this amazing woman closer.

"Morning." Julia raised her warm hazel eyes at her. "How was your sleep?"

"Good." Jackie stretched her sore muscles. After yesterday's mission and long flight, she felt she needed more rest.

Julia gave her a polite smile and poured a glass of milk. "Here. This is our traditional Holiday breakfast. I know it's a bit early to celebrate, but since you're here only for a week, why not try it?"

"Thank you." Jackie took a sip from her glass. The milk was fresh and still warm. It was probably just delivered from the local farm. Its taste was sweet and times better than any ice-cream she had tried in Middle Lake. Sometimes she missed this simplicity of life in a small town. However, her life was in a different place now.

"How was your mission?" Julia asked.

The memory of the dead girl, Carry, arose before her eyes, and Jackie choked on the milk. She put her glass aside and started coughing.

Julia patted her back. "Is everything okay?"

Jackie wiped her lips with the napkin that Julia gave her. "Sort of. I just wish I could forget about work for one day."

"It's never that easy." Julia gave her a small smile in understanding. "Theo said it was another victim, but you managed to find the culprit."

"It's true," Jackie said. Considering that Theo couldn't reveal too much information because the culprit was Julia's mother-in-law, she must be careful with her word choice. Last night they followed that woman, Claudia Turner, to the motel where she stopped for the night. Theo warned the motel owner to notify him immediately if the woman moved out. This morning he was supposed to send the letters to warn all the Guardian Houses about her.

As all their team agreed, it was the only reliable way – to keep an eye on Claudia Turner to find the cult and other prospective suspects and victims. "Is Theo gone already?"

Julia nodded. "He woke early and left before sunrise. But he must be back this afternoon."

"Great. I think we all need to have some fun besides work."

"Like what?"

"How about a snow battle?"

Julia laughed, her cheeks flushing. "It's a lovely idea. And it must be snowing later today."

"But it's sunny." Jackie glanced at the window that opened a view to the bright snowy yard. A beautiful blue sky was decorated with puffy, fast-flowing clouds.

"When it's windy, everything changes fast."

She took a bite of a cookie. It was melting in her mouth. "I love this! Is it your family recipe?"

Julia shook her head. "Actually, I inherited it from Kyle's mom."

Jackie fought the urge to spit out the dough.

"When we were kids," Julia continued, "Mrs. Turner baked them on Holiday week and sent the boxes to the families who supported the Divine community. It was like opening a gift!"

Jackie gave her a worried look. "Did you see her recently?"

"Not really." Julia sat on a stool. "Why do you ask?"

She looked around, making sure that no one was eavesdropping. "This Divine community that you named... It might be connected to the case we are investigating. I thought Mrs. Turner might mention something if you talked to her."

Julia placed her palm on her chest, breathing heavily. "I don't know. Honestly, I haven't seen her much since that tragedy with Kyle's sister. She didn't even come to our wedding. But this summer, we had our own loss..." Her hand lowered to her belly, and her eyes filled with tears.

Jackie gave her a clean kitchen towel. "I'm so sorry about that."

She wiped her tears and continued. "After the miscarriage, I was in bed all week. Once, I woke up in the middle of the night and went downstairs to get some water. Mrs. Turner was in the kitchen, waiting for me. As I figured, she came to support me right after she learned the sad news."

"Did Kyle ask her to visit?"

"No. As I figured, Mrs. Turner had learned about it from someone in our church. She said not to tell anyone about her visit, even Kyle."

"What else did she tell you?"

"She was so... preoccupied. She seemed too worried about my well-being." Julia shivered. "And she said such weird things. That the balance of life and death must be restored. She vowed to take care of it."

Jackie took a heavy breath. Everything matched. Mrs. Turner visited Julia in the summer, and the ritual killings started in September. Most likely, Mrs. Turner was the one who killed these girls herself. Of course, her guilt had to be proved, but now Jackie had more pieces to this puzzle.

"The morning after her visit... I was so fuzzy. Honestly, I thought it was just a dream." Julia pulled her hand under the collar of her dress and revealed a star amulet. "But she gave me this, proving our meeting was real."

"What's that?" Jackie asked, glancing at the silver star with crystal incrustation. It had five sharp ends, and four of them shimmered with inner Lights of different shades. *Do these Lights belong to the victims?* Creeps ran down her spine as Jackie imagined that a particle of Carry's soul was trapped in one of the crystals.

"Mrs. Turner said to wait for five months to have the soul of the lost baby returned to me," Julia explained. "In the beginning, I didn't believe it, but each month after the full moon rises, one of the star endings lights up. I can't explain it. But I keep wearing it. Sometimes, when I feel sad and distressed, I just look at it, and it fills my heart with hope."

No doubt, it's black magic. Jackie dropped her head in her palms. Occult science was officially forbidden in Lake Kingdoms. In the Academy, she read about some rituals just to learn why they were prohibited. The mages who crossed this line thought they could bring souls back to life. However, the price was too high. There were multiple registered cases of childbirth when newborns suffered from incurable diseases. In fact, this soul-summoning ritual didn't really save anyone. Instead, it sentenced these children to a new life full of suffering. In many cases, such babies died at an early age, and some lived to an older age but experienced a lot of pain.

This is why such practices were forbidden – they were inhuman and just cruel. Yes, it was hard to let go of people who passed away, especially children, but death was a natural life extension. Humans had to respect their circle of life. At least to try to find a way through grieving and rituals to honor the memory of the ones who were no longer alive. If only there was a way to explain it to the mother who lost her child...

"How do you feel now?" Jackie asked in a weak voice.

Julia shrugged. "I don't know. I just want to do everything as usual. This sadness sometimes distracts me, but I think I'll handle it." She hesitated and hid her amulet back. "Sorry, I don't even know why I told you this. Maybe it's because of the letter."

"Which letter?"

"The one that you asked Kyle to write to me."

Jackie nodded, remembering their interview. "I'm glad you read it."

"I liked it, and know you're worried about me. But I'll be alright. After all, I feel stronger each month, and this morning the fourth ending started shining. I have a feeling that in a month, something exciting will happen."

"What if it won't be as exciting as you expect?"

Julia rose and gave her an irritated look. "It will, okay?! And if you don't believe me, that's fine. I know better, after all."

Jackie gave her a look full of regrets. Three years ago, Julia saved her life, and even though their acquaintance was brief, she seemed to be a different person back then – compassionate and soft. Now, she was wounded and full of suppressed anger. Which meant that it was better not to argue. "Please, don't be mad. I believe you."

Julia calmed a bit. "Good. So what's the deal with Mrs. Turner?"

"Nothing." Jackie lied. "She seems to be a nice woman."

Julia cocked her head. "But...?"

Jackie moved her hand along the table. "But did you check what kind of magic she might use on you?"

"What do you mean?" Julia frowned. "Mrs. Turner does it from the heart, which means I can trust it."

"Well, if I were you, I would double-check. You know, some amulets can do more harm –"

"You are not me!" Julia stomped her foot in impatience.

The sound of the opening door interrupted the scene, and they turned to the entrance doors. Kyle walked in, his cheeks beet red from the morning frost. He hung his coat on a hanger near the entrance and stepped into the kitchen. "Is everything alright?"

"Not really." Julia kept piercing Jackie with her narrowed eyes. "Honey, please tell our guests to mind their own business. I'm getting really exhausted from their presence." Without waiting for a reply, she turned and walked upstairs to her bedroom.

When her steps got quiet, Kyle sat near Jackie. "Listen, I know how much you want to help, and I appreciate everything you did. But we just sorted it out with Julia. In the morning, she felt so calm. Maybe we shouldn't open this topic again."

She lowered her voice. "I'm afraid we must open it. It's worse than I thought, Kyle."

"Why?"

"She might be under a bad influence." She sighed, unable to tell the whole truth. "Did you see her amulet? A five-beam star?"

He shrugged. "Maybe. I didn't pay close attention."

"It's black magic. Do you know what it means?"

"Not really." His face became concerned.

"She is on the way to bring the baby's soul back."

His eyes widened, but he didn't utter a word.

"Julia doesn't seem to know about it and the consequences," Jackie explained. "But I must stop the person who gave her this occult amulet."

"You know who gave it to her?"

Jackie swallowed. Again, it was too risky to reveal the truth. "I have some ideas. Meanwhile, you will need to warn Julia."

He rolled his eyes. "Like that will work."

"Of course not," she agreed. "But if Julia 'accidentally' finds the information with this ritual, she might start doubting it."

"Accidentally? What is that supposed to mean?"

Jackie leaned closer. "I mean in the book, preferably with this amulet drawing. If it lies on your nightstand on the right page, she might get suspicious and read this. This is how she will learn the truth."

"And where will we get such a book?"

"I'll look in the library."

He gave her a doubtful look. "Who will give you a forbidden manuscript?"

Jackie gave him a sly smile. "Fortunately, I know one sneaky librarian."

17

Under the Veil

After a late lunch, Elisa walked out of the house and stopped on the porch. The wind had calmed, but heavy clouds covered the sky. She extended her hand, watching as a snowflake landed on her black glove. This snowflake was perfectly shaped, with six sparkling points and a peculiar square in the middle. Its beauty was both precious and fragile, much like love and life itself. *Why does everything here remind me of loss?*

Jackie approached and hugged her from behind. "Julia was right about the weather change."

"But not about the way she treated you," Elisa said, frowning. Their morning quarrel had woken her up, but Julia was gone by the time she came downstairs.

"Please, let's not talk about it. I feel so bad for being such a nasty guest."

Elisa sighed. In the morning, she had done her best to comfort everyone after that conflict, and now she could finally spend some alone time with her beloved woman. It would be silly to waste this precious time discussing Kyle's family. "Agreed. What do you want to do?"

"What do people do here in such weather?"

"There are many winter activities in this town. On the central plaza, we have a skating rink –"

Jackie let out a heavy sigh, indicating that they had already done enough activities the day before and both needed time to rest.

"Or we can simply take a walk in the park," Elisa suggested. "I promised to show you the bridge of wishes."

Jackie smiled. "Sounds good to me."

They walked along the familiar alleys that Elisa had known since she was a little girl. It felt strange to realize that she was now an adult, with new worries and responsibilities filling her life. And now, her life was intertwined with Jackie's. Her true love walked beside her, admiring the beauty of the tree branches covered in a thin layer of snow.

"I'm so sorry," Elisa said. "About Carry and the ruined vacation."

"It's not your fault that someone decided to kill her. But I'll do my best to help you."

"What do you mean?"

"I've decided to take a key role in the further investigation."

"What?!" Elisa stopped walking. "Absolutely not."

Jackie took Elisa's hands in hers. "Listen, I didn't say anything at home, but something bad is happening to Julia."

"She mentioned her loss to me," Elisa said. "I think we just need to give her more time and space."

"It's not just that," Jackie whispered. "I talked to her in the morning and learned the terrible truth. It's worse than I thought. Much, much worse."

Elisa dropped her hands. "Okay, now you're scaring me."

Jackie looked into her eyes. "Julia met Claudia, or as she called her, Mrs. Turner, in the summer. Claudia gave her an occult amulet that is used to summon lost souls."

"Why are you saying such nonsense?" Elisa took off one of her gloves to check Jackie's forehead. Her temperature seemed normal, ruling out the possibility of a fever or illness that could cause delusions. "Are you feeling alright?"

Jackie touched her hand and lowered it. "Yes, I'm sober and conscious. When I talked to Julia, I saw this amulet with my own eyes."

"Did you mention that it's a terrible idea to summon the baby's soul?"

"Of course!" Jackie waved her hands. "But she didn't believe it!"

Elisa frowned, processing the information. "So, Mrs. Turner attempted to bring back her grandchild through black magic, and her daughter-in-law is so consumed by grief that she doesn't realize she's cursing her future child to a life of suffering?"

"Exactly," Jackie confirmed.

Elisa gasped. "All these sacrifices... she's doing it... for Julia?"

Jackie nodded. "Yes. And we're running out of time – Claudia needs just one more victim to complete her collection. I'm certain that many vulnerable young women in Middle Lake could fall under her influence. We need to act swiftly before it's too late."

Elisa shook her head. "We need to plan an undercover operation. While we may not have enough female guardians, we could potentially recruit someone from the engineering department. I'll start considering suitable candidates."

"Well, initially, it will take time to get everything in place and organized. At least a week. That's a quarter of our remaining time, which is too much. Secondly, I could play this role perfectly as I have extensive knowledge of domestic violence. I believe no actress could portray this role as authentically as I could." Jackie gave her a pleading look. "Please, let me help you and Julia."

Elisa cursed under her breath. She was willing to go to the cult herself without hesitation, but the issue was that Mrs. Turner knew her. Furthermore, this woman was a mind-reader, possessing the same Gift as Jackie. This alignment was advantageous because Mrs. Turner wouldn't immediately discern Jackie's true intentions – similar Gifts didn't work against each other. Additionally, Jackie could leverage this to infiltrate the cult and gather more information from within. Despite Elisa's reluctance to put Jackie in harm's way and disrupt their vacation, this plan seemed logical. Jackie was the ideal candidate for this mission.

"Fine," Elisa said through clenched teeth.

Jackie smiled and hugged her. "Thank you. It will all work out, I promise!"

Elisa glanced over her shoulder through the falling snow. At the end of the alley, the bridge of wishes sparkled with crystals of time, now glowing in a bright yellow hue like miniature suns. Elisa took Jackie's hand. "Come on, let's do something special."

Jackie gave her a curious look and followed her down the alley.

The old bridge connected two banks of the frozen river, its gray stones dusted with a layer of snow. Yellow crystals of time adorned the metal railings. Elisa and Jackie climbed onto the bridge and paused in the middle.

Elisa ran her hand along the railing, brushing off the snow. "According to the old legend, if you make a wish here, it will come true. But it must be sincere."

"Have you made your wish?"

Elisa shook her head. "It's a once-in-a-lifetime opportunity."

"Hmm…" Jackie touched the icy-cold railings. "If I had just one wish, I wouldn't waste it either."

"Maybe now is a good moment to make it," Elisa said, taking Jackie's hands in hers and gazing into her eyes. "All I want is to be with you. Always. Whatever happens next."

Jackie squeezed her palms. "Me too. Wherever we go, I want to be by your side. I want to keep falling in love with you every day."

"And I want to keep falling in love with you." Elisa smiled, trying to push back tears of joy. "Gee, it sounds like a wedding vow."

"Maybe it is the vow." Jackie leaned closer, almost brushing her lips against Elisa's. "I know our union isn't officially recognized, but I love you too much to care about the law."

"It's strange to hear this from a lawyer," Elisa teased.

"I once heard that we can change human law."

"We can try," Elisa whispered. "But it won't be easy."

Jackie lowered her voice. "Like we've ever chosen the easiest path."

"Then it's settled," Elisa said. "Do you agree to be my wife in all the joys and troubles that life brings us?"

"I do." Jackie smiled. "What about you?"

"Of course I do."

For a moment, the crystals of time seemed to vibrate and shine brighter. *Is it just a trick of the imagination?* Elisa pondered. Whatever it was, it felt so right and peaceful that she was willing to believe that Divine itself had blessed their love.

As they walked back home, darkness descended upon the town. The snow had ceased, and the waning moon peeked through the lazily drifting clouds. Elisa held Jackie's hand tightly, as if releasing it would cause the magic of the day to vanish. She dreaded the thought of meeting Theo and the necessity of strategizing their next steps to apprehend the cult members. If she could, she would linger in this moment forever, savoring the delicate beauty of their bond. While it might not be recognized by others, it was undeniably real for the two of them, and that was all that truly mattered.

Upon reaching the porch, Jackie halted. "You seem troubled."

Elisa shrugged. "It's... nothing. I just wish I could prolong this day."

Jackie gave her a mischievous look. "Luckily, I know how to lift your spirits." With that, she leaned to the side of the path, scooping up some snow and compacting it into a snowball.

Elisa raised her hand in warning. "Don't you dare!"

Ignoring Elisa's words, Jackie playfully threw a snowball at her shoulder.

Elisa brushed the snow off her coat and retaliated by grabbing some snow of her own. "That's it! I'll teach you not to disrespect your wife!"

My wife. This term settled warmly in her chest. Jackie chuckled and took a couple of steps back, evading Elisa's throw. "Sorry, wife, but your aim is really questionable."

Elisa formed a new snowball in her hands. "I'm going to get you!"

"Oh no!" Jackie widened her eyes in mock fear and retreated to the yard.

Laughing, they chased each other around the front yard until their friends emerged to join in the fun. Theo was the first to come out, followed by Kyle and even Julia.

After the snowball fight, all five of them lay on their backs, catching their breath.

"What was that?" Theo inquired.

Elisa turned to him and playfully poked his shoulder. "Just having some fun. Did you forget what that is?"

"I think we all forgot," Kyle chimed in.

Julia turned to Jackie, her eyes shimmering in the moonlight. "I'm sorry for what I said this morning. I was too tense."

"It's okay," Jackie replied with a gentle smile. "I suppose this day was a good reminder that we're not too old and not too hopeless."

18

A Crossroad

The trail, covered with a fresh layer of snow powder, was soft and pleasant to ride on. Jackie halted her horse at the crossroad sign. Here, a wider road led to Middle Lake and a smaller one to the motel where Claudia Turner, the suspect, had stayed for the night. According to their informants, Claudia was expected to return on the road that day.

Jackie checked the time crystal on her bracelet. *Yellow.* It meant that their paths would cross in less than half an hour. She dismounted her horse and inspected the saddle. The billet strap, a belt connecting the sides of the saddle through the horse's belly, was almost new. Jackie replaced it with the old, worn-out one, causing the saddle to slightly lean to the side.

"Here we go. A damsel in distress and her troublesome journey shall soon begin," she said, patting the horse's muzzle with a smile. "Now, let's grab something to eat."

The horse neighed in agreement, and Jackie took some hay from her road bag to feed her.

Claudia didn't keep them waiting for too long. Her silhouette, cloaked in black, appeared on the horizon in about twenty minutes. She rode the same horse, now without the victim's body and without a cart, indicating that she had likely rented it previously.

Jackie rubbed her eyes to make her face appear puffy. To make the right first impression, she needed to look like a naive girl who had escaped from home and gotten into trouble in the middle of the forest.

As Claudia rode closer, she stopped and dismounted onto the snowy path. Her hood fell off, revealing her blue eyes. She gave Jackie a pitiful look. "Poor thing! What happened to you?"

Jackie suppressed the urge to accuse Claudia of the murders right away. According to the plan, Claudia needed to lead her to the cult, and only then would Jackie have the satisfaction of bringing her to justice.

"My saddle seems to have broken," Jackie said in the saddest voice she could master.

Claudia glanced at her horse and frowned. Hopefully, she had some extra saddle parts with her, as any normal traveler would. "Why are you traveling alone?" Claudia inquired.

I was waiting for this question! Faking a heavy sigh and lowering her eyes, she replied, "I'm so stupid, that's why."

"Don't ever say that."

"But I am! I... I... deserved it!" Jackie sobbed dramatically. "Maybe I should just freeze to death on this path!"

Moved by Jackie's distress, Claudia approached and offered her a clean handkerchief. "Please, calm down and talk to me."

Jackie accepted the handkerchief and wiped the corners of her eyes before continuing her performance.

"I'm so sorry," Jackie said. "I got so upset and I have no idea where to go."

Claudia gave her a curious look. "Why aren't you going home?"

Jackie paused, biting her lower lip. It was crucial to proceed with caution and not reveal her fake home location too quickly, as it could raise suspicion. She continued to play her part carefully, recounting the fabricated story developed by the guardian team. "I... I can't go home anymore. I broke off an engagement that my father arranged, and I had to leave. I wanted to go to the capital, Middle Lake, to find work and support myself. But now, I feel so sorry for what I've done to them."

Claudia nodded in understanding. "Let's address the most urgent matter first."

Jackie looked at her with gratitude as Claudia smiled and retrieved a new leather billet strap from her roadbag. Then, she rolled up her sleeves and swiftly began fixing Jackie's horse saddle with precision and speed.

While Claudia was working, Jackie took a moment to inhale the frosty forest air, relishing the return to undercover work after years as a lawyer. The thrill of deceiving the criminal filled her heart with excitement, though she remained mindful of the risks, moving cautiously like a crouching tiger. Perhaps she should ask Elisa to involve her in missions more frequently; they made a formidable team.

"What's your name?" Claudia's question interrupted Jackie's thoughts. She finished her work and rolled her sleeves back.

"Jackie," she replied with a shy smile.

"I'm Claudia." Wiping her forehead, Claudia took a step back, admiring her handiwork. "See, it's not the end of the world. Now you can continue your journey."

Jackie blinked, taken off-guard. She didn't expect Claudia would let her go so easily. Jackie decided to improvise. "Thank you so much, Claudia," she said, reaching into her purse. "I have several coins to pay for your kindness."

Claudia laughed. "Keep them for yourself, child. You may need the money on your journey."

"Thank you," Jackie replied, unable to conceal her frustration. *Will Claudia simply leave and miss the opportunity to lure me into the cult? Was my performance too pushy?*

Claudia returned to her horse and stood beside it, observing Jackie with narrowed eyes. It was evident that she was deliberating a decision. *What will it be?* Jackie's muscles tensed in anticipation.

"By the way, I'm heading to Middle Lake as well," Claudia announced. "We will be safer together, and I would appreciate your company."

Jackie breathed a sigh of relief. While she had been contemplating how to lure Claudia into her trap, Claudia seemed to be employing her own tactics to draw closer. This week was shaping up to be quite intriguing.

"Ah, that would be lovely!" Jackie replied.

Closer to sunset, they arrived at a large road motel. Inside, the wooden hall was adorned with antique chandeliers, and several tables occupied by visitors lined the windows. Jackie, who typically preferred sleeping under the stars, was taken aback by the opulence of the place.

With her mouth slightly agape in awe, Jackie surveyed the surroundings as she followed Claudia to the registration desk. Claudia requested a room with two beds, and the receptionist handed them two keys before stating the price, causing Jackie to gasp.

Claudia flashed her a cheerful smile. "Don't worry. It's nothing for me."

"I just don't want to be a burden," Jackie replied. Turning to the receptionist, a young man in a pristine white shirt, she added, "I can sleep in the stables."

The receptionist glanced at Claudia and then back at Jackie. "Sorry, we have too many horses vying for rest there. I'm afraid human company might disturb them."

Claudia laughed and waved her hand. "Oh, I love your jokes, Sammy!"

Jackie forced a silly smile. In this lavish hall of the luxury motel, she felt like a powerless stranger, unable to control her own fate. It was clear that Claudia had used this manipulation tactic on all her victims, trapping them in a debt they could never repay. This tactic was designed to make them feel indebted to her. *What a deceitful game she played!* Suppressing her aversion, Jackie replied aloud, "Thank you, Claudia."

In the room, Jackie's "debt" continued to grow. Claudia ordered a lavish dinner consisting of thick fish soup, freshly baked garlic bread, a fresh vegetable salad, and, for dessert, an apple pie accompanied by two shots of cherry brandy. The cost of the meal, along with half of the room's expenses, amounted to a quarter of what Jackie earned in a month as a lawyer.

As the servant girl set the dishes on the table, Jackie looked out the window. The darkness outside enveloped the street, and the candlelight flickered on the heavy dark-burgundy curtains.

Once the dinner was served, Jackie approached the table and took a seat, perching on the edge of her chair.

Claudia refrained from touching the food immediately. Instead, she extended both her hands to Jackie. "Let's pray."

Jackie took Claudia's cold palms in hers and closed her eyes, focusing on Claudia's voice. She recognized the prayer and repeated the words along with Claudia.

"Thank you, sacred Light of Divine!
For the warmth of our shelter,
For the roof above our heads,
For this amazing food on our table.
Bless the people who prepared all of it for us."

After the prayer, they opened their eyes and began to eat. Jackie realized just how hungry she was, but she made a conscious effort to match Claudia's pace, taking small bites of food.

Claudia sipped her soup elegantly from her polished spoon. "So, Jackie, how much working experience do you have?"

Jackie shrugged, focusing on recalling her fabricated backstory. "Well, back in our village, I helped organize events for the local church."

Claudia raised an eyebrow. "Churches aren't typically bustling with paid positions; they usually rely on volunteers for support. It may not be what you're seeking."

"As long as they provide food and shelter, I'm willing to take on any job," Jackie replied, injecting enthusiasm into her fake plan. "There are also hotels, schools, and other communities where I could potentially find work."

Claudia rested her chin on her hand thoughtfully. "Honestly, I'm starting to believe that our meeting was divinely orchestrated."

It was. And it includes your arrest. Jackie gave her a curious look. "What makes you think so?"

Claudia's voice was as sweet as a potion. "You're one of the kindest young women I've ever met. You are modest and polite. I have a small religious community, and you might be a perfect fit."

Jackie swallowed her bread, maintaining a facade of innocence to conceal her true intentions. "Really?"

Claudia nodded. "Now I see it clearly. And the best part is that you have already done this kind of job. Where did you say it was?"

Jackie had never mentioned the location of her fabricated home before, but now it was time to reveal this detail. "In Edenville. It's a small town after the Crystal Caves."

Claudia's eyes gleamed with a predator glint. "I've always wanted to visit that town. People say it's a very special place."

Indeed, a very special place where victim number five was meant to meet her death. Jackie cleared her throat, feigning excitement. "I can't believe someone like you would be interested in such a small, remote town."

"Trust me, I am." Claudia laughed, the long shadows dancing along her cheekbones.

Jackie nearly dropped her spoon. This woman was as intimidating as hell itself. The knot in her stomach tightened, and she looked at the food, finding it impossible to take another bite. The burgundy glass of brandy, resembling blood in the dim light, seemed like the most appealing option. Jackie raised the shot, forcing a fake smile. "For dreams to come true!"

Claudia raised her shot in agreement, and they both drank.

As the dinner came to an end, Jackie gazed out into the darkness. The twisted bushes quivered in the night wind, frozen in place. She silently moved her lips, offering a prayer for Elisa, hoping that she was having a better night.

19

The Old News

"But I need this book," Elisa pleaded. She stood at the reception desk, facing her old friend Laura, who refused to cooperate.

"I can't help you with this," Laura said, crossing her arms over her chest, her brown eyes merciless. "There is a reason why black magic is strictly forbidden. If the sacred manuscript ends up in the wrong hands, it might lead to severe disaster."

"It has already ended up in the wrong hands!" Elisa exclaimed, starting to lose her patience. "This is why I need this damn book – to show it to my friend to stop her from making this disastrous step!"

Laura shook her head. "Still no."

Elisa let out a frustrated moan. This conversation was leading nowhere and was exhausting her. She had honestly thought that Laura would help because they were old friends.

She still worked part-time in the library of the Guardian Academy while studying in college. This job helped Laura pay for her education and gave her access to all her study books. She was the only person who could help Elisa with this part of her mission.

"Is this all you've got?" Elisa asked in her best sarcastic tone. "What about your 'smart people can go beyond the rules' thing?"

She sighed. "Okay, I might have said that when I just started this job. But now I have too much at stake. I need to take care of my reputation."

"Reputation?!" Elisa smirked. "How ethical is it to let someone become a victim of black magic knowing that you had a chance to prevent it?"

Laura paused, thinking. Then she moved away from the reception desk. "Wait here," she said before disappearing between the rows of paper archives.

Elisa sank into a large visitor's chair, her mind shrouded in fog.

She touched a beautiful kettle, its clay walls still warm. When she was studying here, it had become their ritual – for Laura, Jackie, and Elisa. They would gather once a week, drinking tea, eating candies, and discussing the latest news. *How quickly times change!*

Now, it seemed they were walking three different paths. Two years ago, Laura had started studying literature, with her original plan being to become a teacher. She had taken a course in journalism out of curiosity and a challenge to try writing. There, she had fallen in love. Journalism turned out to be a perfect fit for Laura – she was constantly surrounded by rumors, and she could write about her favorite topics with flair. Her articles were well-received by readers. Laura enjoyed the routine and being close to famous people and interesting events. She was now about to graduate and had already signed a contract with the local newspaper that spread news across all of Middle Lake city and its suburbs.

Of course, there were things she had to let go of. These were her final days at The Academy as a librarian, and soon she would be moving on with her life. The new opportunity also ignited her desire to build a life in the capital, distancing her from Theo, who preferred the quiet town of Triville. It led to their eventual breakup. Surprisingly, the end of their relationship went smoothly, and now both of them were fully focused on their work.

The sound of footsteps, accompanied by the rustle of papers, shook Elisa from her thoughts. Laura was walking back to her, holding a pile of old newspapers in her hands. Elisa rose to her feet and rushed to help her.

"What's that?" Elisa asked as she took half of the newspapers. *Who knew that news could weigh so much?* With so many of them, it felt like she was holding a bunch of logs.

Laura placed her pile on the coffee table and wiped her forehead. "This is what can save Julia."

"*Old news?*" Elisa asked as she placed her pile on the chair.

"Exactly. Everything you told me reminded me of an unusual case we discussed in class. It was an interview that a journalist conducted with a woman who had gone through a soul-summoning ritual. She spoke about a pentagram amulet and how happy she was about her newborn baby. Then she shared her regrets when the baby fell seriously ill and passed away. After the funeral, she was shattered. Her guide advised her to write down the story and share it with someone to help overcome her grief."

"And she published it in a newspaper?"

"Not right away. When she sent it to newspapers, hoping to warn other women not to fall into the same trap, the major newspapers weren't interested in her story. So she found one publisher, who agreed only because his journal was on the verge of shutting down."

"So it was eventually printed?"

Laura nodded. "Not just printed. It actually sparked the creation of a new column, 'Old News.' Essentially, the journal published stories that had happened several years ago. Surprisingly, people enjoyed it, and the journal continued to thrive. In fact, it has become very popular and has even won awards for this column."

"Well, that's very impressive," Elisa remarked. "But what about Julia?"

"Show her this article," Laura said, as if it were an obvious solution.

"You think it would work?"

"Of course. I know you wanted to give her a textbook, but honestly, educational books are not always persuasive. People read them but often fail to grasp all the hidden opportunities or, in our case, consequences. On the other hand, real human stories are a natural way of sharing essential life experiences," Laura explained, giving Elisa a look of someone experienced in dealing with a novice. "Okay, let's simplify it. People like to have theoretical knowledge, but we learn best through practice. Does that make more sense to you?"

"Yes," Elisa said, recalling her experiences as a guardian. Whatever she had planned or thought through while studying paled in comparison to dealing with real investigations.

"This is why we tell children fairy tales. The stories help them 'live through experiences' in their imagination. Even though they are not real, they help build morals and guide better future choices when facing life's obstacles."

"This is exactly what Julia needs," Elisa said, smiling enthusiastically. "Let's find this story then!"

They scrolled through papers one after the other, their eyes scanning the titles. Finally, after half an hour, Elisa held the paper with the article in her hands. It only took up half of the newspaper page, but if Laura was right, this story meant a great deal. She pressed the newspaper to her chest. "Thank you, dear. I knew you would help us."

"I'm glad we found a better way than stealing from a secret archive," Laura said with a smile. "I hope you know that the story is only the beginning. It may help her see things differently, but she will likely need professional help to heal."

"Jackie already mentioned that," Elisa said, folding the paper and tucking it into her road bag. "It was actually her original idea to bring Julia into her female circle program. From what I understand, it's been quite effective."

"Jackie is a brilliant mind-reader who has used her Gift so wisely," Laura remarked as she began cleaning up the mess and organizing the papers by date before stacking them neatly. "How is she, by the way? I haven't seen her in ages."

"She's doing very well." Elisa smiled. "We recently visited the dragon farm and even had the opportunity to fly with Rose. It was an incredible vacation."

Laura froze with the paper in her hand, her voice turning quiet. "I truly miss those adorable dragons."

Elisa bit her tongue. *Why did I bring up the dragons?* It only reminded Laura of Theo. He was the one who had taken their breakup well, not her. "Sorry. I didn't mean to upset you."

"It's okay," Laura said, continuing to work on arranging the news. "I suppose that's what happens when you break up with someone after several years. We still have mutual friends and so many shared memories. And we always will. I just hope he'll find his happy ending."

"Me too," Elisa agreed. She really hoped that Theo would find his true love. But as for now, he simply was avoiding Laura. Today, Elisa and Theo had arrived in Middle Lake together on his dragon, but he had chosen not to join her in visiting the library. Instead, he had arranged a meeting with Urchin. She understood his decision, as she had once been in his shoes. Theo was a heart-breaker, but he didn't want to make things harder for Laura. "It always takes time to recover. Any connection will weaken if you don't nurture it."

"True." Laura nodded. She had finished organizing the papers, and the room was now clean again, just the way she liked it. "How about a cup of tea? We have an hour before the cadets fill the library to prepare for their finals."

"I'm in!" Elisa chuckled. "Damn, it feels so good not to be a cadet anymore."

20

Daughters of Divine

The building where the cult members lived was nothing like she expected. When Jackie finally arrived in the suburbs of Middle Lake with Claudia, they stopped at a shabby two-story wooden building near the church. The paint that used to be white was now cracked, revealing old wooden planks. The windows were narrow and small, probably to retain warmth inside the house.

On the path to the house, they dismounted their horses.

"Here is where the girls live," Claudia explained.

Jackie mustered a smile. "And you will live here with us?"

"I prefer living in my own home." She pointed at the church building – two gorgeous towers connected with a hall for visitors. Both towers had shining golden roofs decorated with crystal stars, symbolizing eternal Divine Light. Now, these stars were dull as the day was murky and cloudy.

The groom approached them, and Jackie let him take her horse to the stables. Then she turned to Claudia. "Do all the girls have horses?"

She shook her head. "Here we share. Just ask the groom or church servant if you need something, and they will be glad to help you."

Jackie frowned. If she decided to escape this cult, it would be tricky – even though there was a village nearby, it was at least a two-hour ride to the capital. To take a horse, she had to face Claudia's loyal servants, who might warn her. Well, it was convenient for Claudia – she kept everything under control. It also meant that it was better to find other ways of escape.

"What's wrong?" Claudia asked suspiciously.

Her voice made Jackie startle. Her observations would have to wait until she was alone. Otherwise, she risked losing her trust. "Nothing. I just like riding."

"We don't encourage long rides. Usually, we are very busy."

Busy with killing vulnerable women, Jackie thought. "What will be my job?" she asked aloud.

"I'll show you." Claudia took her by the elbow, and they walked to the small building.

An antique fireplace was burning in a spacious hall room, filling the house with warmth. Two young women, wearing black woolen dresses and white aprons, moved inside, dusting the shelves and fluffing the cushions. Upon noticing Claudia, they both dropped their activities and bowed in greeting.

Claudia smiled at them. "Good morning! Welcome our new daughter, Jackie."

Jackie flinched. Usually, older church members referred to visitors as 'sons' or 'daughters', and the way Claudia used the same names for her circle of murderers was disturbing.

The young women came closer. The first one was in her twenties with a long black plait and olive skin. "I am Margaret," she said, giving Jackie a warm hug.

Jackie closed her eyes, using the moment of physical touch. Her Mind-reading Gift quickly found a connection with Margaret's memories, and she was... spotless. Margaret spent most of her time doing housework, helping in the kitchen, and praying.

Jackie stepped back, hoping to have better luck with the second woman.

"Anna," she introduced herself. The woman had a deep, sad voice and dull blue eyes. When her gaze met Jackie's, she turned away. *Is she shy or avoiding my touch on purpose?*

"Anna is not too communicative," Claudia explained with a soft smile. She then touched Margaret's shoulder. "So, Margaret is the oldest Daughter. She is in charge here when I'm absent. She will show you the rooms and give you new clothes."

"Thank you," Jackie said.

"I'll see you all at dinner," Claudia promised before leaving.

The old and squeaky stairs led to the upper floor. Here were the five bedrooms and one washroom. All the doors were half-open, and Jackie craned her head to glance inside. The bedrooms were perfectly clean, with the beds well-made. There were no other girls inside, which meant they were all busy with their work.

Margaret stopped at the room at the end of the corridor and pushed the door. Jackie walked inside. There were two beds covered with soft beige blankets. She resisted the urge to fall into bed immediately and catch some rest after the long road. Instead, she turned to Margaret. "So you share the bedrooms?"

She nodded. "We share everything – this house, food, duties. You'll be sharing this room with Anna. You just met her in the hall room."

Jackie nodded, remembering the shy blond girl. "Right. She's come here recently, too."

Margaret narrowed her dark-brown eyes. "How do you know?"

Jackie bit her tongue. *From reading your memories, where else?* This girl was too attentive and could create trouble once she learned that Jackie was deceiving them all.

"You look very confident," Jackie flattered her ego, hoping it would help soften her. "Like you've been here for a long time."

"For five years. And during them, I saw a lot of women like you." Margaret gave her a judgmental look, making Jackie feel like she wasn't good enough for their perfect little cult. Not that Jackie cared about settling here, but still, it was unpleasant. "Listen, we try to help the local community and provide work for young women. Unfortunately, most of them have wild dreams, and they don't stay here for too long."

And there is a reason why. Apparently, Margaret wasn't aware of Claudia's plans, which explained why Claudia was traveling alone and killed all the victims herself. "So, what work do you do?" Jackie asked to soothe the pressure between them.

Margaret walked to the closet and revealed a black woolen dress, the same as hers. Then she took a white nightgown. Jackie froze, touching the white material decorated with tiny yellow suns at the collar. In this nightgown, one of the women in this building was supposed to be killed. She put the clothes on the bed and took a seat, fearing she might faint.

"We sewed these clothes ourselves," Margaret explained. "We also cook and bake to help the shelters in Middle Lake city. We make candles and wine; sometimes, the schools invite us to read the psalms and talk to kids."

Jackie smiled. This community seemed to be doing a good thing. Little did Margaret know what was hidden behind this curtain of kindness. "I think I'll love it here."

"You will," Margaret said, relaxing a bit and sitting on the corner of her bed. "And summer is the best. We grow fresh fruits, veggies, and flowers. Do you like flowers?"

"Which girl doesn't?" Jackie laughed. "If it were up to me, I would live in a garden."

"Then you can work with me in the garden this year. I'll show you how to grow roses." Margaret's eyes shone. Damn, she was a good person. Because the eyes never lie. Jackie didn't even need to read her thoughts again to understand it.

"I would love to join you," Jackie said. She was sincere this time. She really would be glad to spend the summer in the rose garden. However, now her job was to find out more details about the next murder. Jackie touched the clothes again, getting used to the sensation of the soft material.

"The black dress is for everyday wear," Margaret clarified. "You will need two or three of them to stay clean before laundry day, which is on Saturday."

Jackie nodded in understanding. "And the white one is for the night?"

Margaret snickered. "Why does everyone think so? No, the white dress is for the ceremonies. We wear it when we have a special event."

A cold shiver ran down her spine. "Which event?"

"Like when we have holiday services or welcome a new Daughter of Divine. This time it's you."

"'Daughters of Divine?' I've never heard of such a name for a religious community."

"Claudia created it," Margaret explained with pride in her voice. "We met five years ago, and she organized all of this." She moved her hand around the room. "This building once was an old motel. People say there was a murder here, so no one wanted to buy this place. Claudia convinced the church to take it. After all, it was very close, and it was just a building. She said that all the good things we do here will clean its negative energy and change its reputation."

Will Claudia's arrest finish this reputation? Jackie wondered. She shook her head to focus on her mission. "It's very smart and might set a good example to others. By the way, when will the ceremony be? For welcoming me as a new Daughter of Divine?"

"It's not that simple. Firstly, you must pass two weeks of probation. So take your time to settle here," Margaret replied, glancing at the time crystal that rested on the nightstand. It was late noon, and its color was yellowish green. She stood up. "Well, I need to finish cleaning, and then we'll have dinner. Have some rest, change, and be ready by six in the evening."

21

The Diary

Dull moonlight illuminated the white ceiling, exposing its imperfect bumps and numerous cracks. Using her imagination, Jackie connected these cracks to form several ugly human faces. However, this activity didn't help her fall asleep. She squirmed in her narrow bed, attempting to find a comfortable position until she faced the wall. She had known from the beginning that she would struggle to be away from Elisa, and now she had no choice but to try to get used to sleeping alone. As Margaret had informed her, this undercover mission could last up to two weeks.

Closing her eyes, Jackie's mind drifted back to the memories of tonight's dinner with Claudia and the other young women residing in the house. There were eight of them, each with her own unique story. Yet, all of their narratives shared a common theme – domestic violence followed by shaming and expulsion from their homes. Sadly, none of the women dared to live on their own terms.

It was as if they had never known any terms beyond those dictated by their communities. It was a tragedy that they resided in a fractured world where kindness was perceived as their greatest weakness.

The bed creaked behind her, causing Jackie to hold her breath and listen intently. Anna, her roommate, rose from the bed and crept towards the corridor. Jackie sat up, glancing at the time crystal. It glowed orange, indicating that it was one in the morning. Jackie waited for a few moments before standing up and venturing out of the room.

In the dark corridor, everything was silent, even the bathroom. *Anna must have gone downstairs.* Considering that Anna had not dressed, she was not planning to leave the house. *What is she doing at such a late hour?*

Jackie cautiously descended the stairs and stood there, observing Anna in the living room. She was engrossed in writing something in a small notebook, the flames from the fireplace casting a glow on her focused expression. *Is it a diary?* Jackie took a step closer, but the creaking of the wooden floor beneath her feet revealed her presence.

Startled, Anna quickly closed her notebook and concealed it behind the pillows. She turned around, asking, "Who's there?"

Taking a deep breath, Jackie walked into the room. There was no point in hiding, as Anna had already noticed her. "Hey, sorry. I didn't mean to startle you. I just wanted to get a glass of water."

Anna gestured towards the kitchen. "It's over there."

"Thank you," Jackie replied with a weary smile before making her way to the kitchen.

As she placed a kettle on the stove, she leaned against the counter, pondering Anna's behavior. Among all the Daughters of Divine, Anna seemed to be the most secretive, and it was beginning to unsettle Jackie.

Jackie had spent the entire evening diligently working towards her mission of uncovering the mysteries of the place. Using her mind-reading Gift, she had managed to delve into the thoughts of almost all the women in the house. However, she encountered difficulty when it came to Anna. This young woman not only avoided physical contact, such as hugs or handshakes, but she also seemed to evade any form of conversation. It was as if Anna was aware of Jackie's Gift and went to great lengths to steer clear of her. *But how could she know?*

Jackie frowned. Perhaps Claudia had discovered her mind-reading Gift. They had held hands multiple times during prayers, and if Claudia had ever attempted to read Jackie's mind, she would have encountered failure, as similar Gifts do not work against each other. It was plausible that Claudia had warned Anna to keep her distance.

The idea of stealing Anna's diary crossed Jackie's mind, tempting her with the possibility of uncovering secrets. But it was a terrible idea. If she were to be caught snooping around, it could lead to suspicions. Perhaps the diary was intentionally hidden as a trap. Jackie resolved not to fall into such a potential trap, at least not before the upcoming ceremony. Patience, though not her strong suit, was crucial in this situation.

As the kettle whistled, Jackie removed it from the stove and opened the kitchen cabinet, retrieving jars of dried herbs such as chamomile and lavender. She also found dried lemon zest, which she added to her drink. After a moment of contemplation, she prepared another cup, this time for Anna. Despite Anna's guarded demeanor, Jackie doubted anyone could refuse a calming drink on such a restless night.

Anna was still engrossed in making notes in the living room when Jackie approached and placed the steaming cup on the coffee table, maintaining a distance to avoid intruding on Anna's personal space. "Here. It helps prevent insomnia," Jackie offered.

Startled, Anna closed her notebook and gave Jackie a surprised look. "Thank you."

"Not a problem," Jackie responded with a shrug, too fatigued to feign niceties or concern. Surprisingly, her aloofness seemed to have an unexpected effect.

"Have a seat," Anna invited, placing her notebook on her lap.

Complying, Jackie settled on the opposite end of the large sofa, which was adorned with a soft blanket. The warmth from the cozy fireplace made it tempting to relax and drift off. Anna smoothed the folds of her nightgown, her gaze lowered. Jackie sensed the awkwardness of the silence but refrained from being the first to speak, unsure of how to initiate a conversation without driving Anna away.

"I'm not very open with new people, sorry," Anna finally said.

"Yeah, I noticed," Jackie quipped, attempting to lighten the mood.

Anna's expression remained serious. "If anyone finds out I have a personal diary, it could lead to trouble."

"Why? Is it forbidden here to write about your feelings?"

Anna blushed. "Claudia instructs me to focus on work. However, at times, my mind is overwhelmed with thoughts, making it difficult to sleep unless I jot them down."

"I can relate. I faced a similar challenge, and my diary helped me navigate through my thoughts when I was recovering from trauma," Jackie shared, offering a supportive gaze. "Don't worry about it. It can be our little secret."

"But Claudia will eventually find out," Anna whispered. "She's a mind reader."

"I assure you, she won't learn it from me," Jackie suggested with a smile.

"Why not?" Anna questioned, batting her eyes. "Are you immune to her Gift?"

Jackie took a sip of her tea, contemplating whether to reveal her ability as a mind reader. If Anna was already aware of Jackie's Gift and testing her, honesty seemed like the best approach to earn her trust. "Exactly. I possess the same Gift, and we are unable to read each other's thoughts."

Anna gasped in surprise. "How interesting."

Like you didn't already know, Jackie thought. Out of loud, she continued the conversation nonchalantly, "You know what? I can help you. There are techniques to conceal information from a mind reader, and I can teach you some tricks."

"Seriously?" Anna looked puzzled. "Why are you helping me?"

"Because it's my duty to aid those in need," Jackie replied, omitting the ulterior motive behind her kindness. Teaching Anna how to create a mental block was essential to prevent Claudia from uncovering their conversation.

"Your duty?" Anna questioned, still uncertain.

Jackie nodded. "I assist women who have faced injustice and strive to rebuild their lives independently."

"Then why are you here as a 'Daughter'? I mean, you could just tell the truth. That you are a teacher."

"A lawyer, actually," Jackie corrected.

"Still, it doesn't explain why you pretend to be one of us," Anna persisted.

Jackie gritted her teeth. It seemed she had no choice but to disclose some information, albeit within limits. Revealing Claudia's involvement as a suspect was out of the question. "Fine, let's make a deal. You share the truth about yourself, and I'll explain why I'm here."

"Then you go first," Anna prompted.

Jackie nodded, prepared to share the fabricated version she had concocted for such a situation. "Your suspicions are correct. It's an investigation, and I'm undercover. One of the missing girls who used to reside here was murdered."

Anna's pure blue eyes widened in shock. "Murdered?!"

"Exactly," Jackie affirmed, not allowing Anna a moment to process the weight of the news she had just shared. Anna's persistent probing had already led Jackie to divulge more than she had intended. "It's a sensitive case, and even Claudia is unaware of the true purpose behind my presence. I must gather evidence to uncover the truth about what happened to this girl."

"Why doesn't Claudia know about your mission?"

Jackie hesitated, unable to disclose the full extent of her investigation. "I don't wish to alarm Claudia with such information and incite panic within this peaceful household. After all, the victim was one of the Daughters, and you all knew her."

"Right." Anna nodded in understanding. "So you've been reading everyone to gather information about this girl?"

"Everyone except you."

Anna shivered and instinctively moved back, creating more distance between them. The revelation seemed to have unsettled her.

"Chill, I'm not going to read you," Jackie reassured Anna wearily. "You already know who I am, so it doesn't make sense. But please, if you have any information about that Daughter, it would be helpful for me to determine the next steps."

"Of course," Anna replied, flipping through the pages of her diary. "I usually make notes on each new girl. Perhaps I knew her. What was her name?"

"Carry. Carry Wilson."

"Here," Anna located the relevant page and began to read aloud.

"November 15th.

I met Carry. She arrived late last night together with Claudia. She appears different from the others – too cheerful, if I may say so. When I first saw her, I wondered why such a lively girl was here. They assigned her to a separate room, isolated. However, there's a thin wall between us, and I can hear her crying at night. Yet, in the morning, she never displays any signs of sadness."

Jackie listened intently, absorbing the details about Carry that Anna had documented in her diary.

"December 3rd.

Carry and Claudia departed together for a conference. It seems that Claudia frequently goes on such trips every month. And why does she always choose a new girl to accompany her?

There are more experienced people here, like Margaret. Well, actually, Margaret's responsibilities within the household likely prevent her from being selected. But she could choose me! I have a strong desire to assist her, and I'll never abandon the community like the other girls she took with her."

Anna closed her notebook and regarded Jackie with a disappointed expression. "Sorry, those were just my thoughts at the time. I was quite emotional."

"Have you ever discussed your interest in participating in Claudia's 'conferences' with her?" Jackie inquired.

Anna nodded. "I questioned her about why she selected newcomers, and she said it was part of a new project, choosing participants randomly. I requested to accompany her next time, and… it was strange," Anna's voice trailed off.

"What did she say?" Jackie prodded, urging Anna to continue.

She shrugged. "She told me that I wasn't ready. She advised me to improve my communication skills if I wanted to be considered for such opportunities."

"Trust me, you have no reason to be envious."

"But I am! I couldn't sleep at night. The more I thought of it, the more I wanted to write something bad about you in my diary," Anna confessed, hugging herself. "And now, after getting to know you, I'm feeling conflicted."

Finishing her tea, Jackie offered a reassuring smile. "Let's set this aside for now, okay? Tomorrow, I'll have a conversation with Claudia regarding the conferences she attended with the missing girls, and I'll proceed from there."

"Missing girls?" Anna's eyes widened in alarm. "How many have gone missing?"

Jackie quickly corrected herself, "I must have misspoken. As far as I know, it was only Carry who disappeared."

Anna blinked, her grip tightening on her diary. "But you're correct. It wasn't just Carry who vanished after their conference. There were at least –"

Jackie interjected, "Let's remember that this is merely a theory that requires verification."

Thankfully, Anna didn't push back. "Will you be joining the conference this time?"

"Perhaps. If everything goes smoothly and you uphold your promise to keep this information confidential."

"I will," Anna affirmed. "Also, you promised to teach me how to create a mental block against mind-reading."

"I did. But first, you need to fulfill your end of the bargain and share more about yourself."

Anna crossed her arms. "My life isn't too interesting."

Jackie settled back on the sofa, relishing its softness. "You'd be surprised how often I've heard that excuse. However, everyone has vulnerabilities that can be exploited, so I need to hear your story to help you develop a mental block."

"Alright," Anna began, her gaze shifting to the fireplace. "I grew up in a small village near High Canyons. I always dreamt of exploring the world and traveling. However, my family arranged a marriage for me right after I completed high school. Faced with a dilemma, I had to choose between marrying a man I didn't love or leaving home to fend for myself. And here I am."

"High school?" Jackie's eyes widened in surprise. "Are you, what, fifteen?"

"Sixteen," Anna corrected. "Old enough to be married and start a family of my own."

Jackie swallowed, processing Anna's revelation. "Most women aren't prepared for such responsibilities at that age, so I empathize with your situation."

Anna sighed. "My parents weren't very understanding. They accused me of being selfish. But is it selfish to desire a life of my own? Even just a small part of it before I become an exhausted mother of six like my own mom?" Tears welled up in her eyes, prompting her to look up and blink them away.

"It's not selfish at all. You made a brave decision to leave that situation. What do you envision for yourself now?"

Anna shrugged. "I've never shared this with anyone. But if you promise to keep it a secret, I'll tell you."

Jackie placed her hand over her heart. "I swear to guard your secret with my life."

Glancing around to ensure no one was eavesdropping, Anna leaned in and whispered, "I wanted to stay here for the winter and then secure a teaching position in Middle Lake. I discovered that I don't require a higher education to teach young children. In the meantime, I planned to save some money and continue my studies."

"Is Claudia aware of your plans?" Jackie inquired.

"Oh, she knows," Anna replied with a smile. "But it's our secret. She advised me not to disclose it to others, as many hold judgments against women exercising their free will. We plan to announce it in the spring before I depart."

"How thoughtful of her," Jackie remarked sarcastically, though Anna didn't seem to notice.

Anna's eyes gleamed with excitement. "Claudia has been incredibly supportive. She offered her help as soon as I shared my plan with her."

Jackie couldn't help but feel a sense of unease about Claudia's actions. If anyone in the house knew about her true nature, it would make it easier for Jackie to expose her. However, based on what she had gleaned from the other girls' thoughts, they all viewed Claudia Turner as a benevolent figure – understanding and supportive. Claudia's manipulation was cunning, as she didn't hesitate to refer to them as her daughters. It was a deceptive ploy. Fortunately, Jackie was adept at manipulation as well. "It's a solid plan," she acknowledged.

Anna offered Jackie a shy smile. "Do you truly believe that?"

She nodded. "Absolutely. While many women prioritize their 'duty,' you have chosen to forge your own path. It deserves respect."

Anna gazed at her intently. "You're incredibly supportive. Thank you for your kind words."

Jackie glanced around discreetly to ensure their conversation remained private. "So, are you prepared to learn some techniques?"

"Always ready," Anna replied with a smile.

22

A Secret

The wax chips were melting in the pot, slowly turning into one liquid mass that Jackie was supposed to stir every minute. She mixed the chips well and placed a wooden spatula on the plate nearby.

This room was in the basement of the church, perfectly quiet and dull. Here, Jackie could use her time to think of her next move. She had been here for two weeks already. So far, all she managed to figure out was that Claudia was the organizer of all the ritual killings and the executioner. However, there was no direct evidence of her crimes. The guardian team who worked on her case in Triville managed to collect only the testimony of the priest who revealed the dark side of this woman and the records of that night when she dropped the body of a dead girl, Carry, at her parents' house. Of course, they could make an arrest right away based on it.

However, there was a big chance that Claudia would refuse to confess to committing the murder. They had no other traces, and all the Daughters of Divine, as Claudia called them, had no idea about the ritual killings.

Jackie stirred the wax again, ensuring it was smooth. She had no other choice but to wait for a chance to follow Claudia and Anna, her next prospective victim, to the next 'conference,' or to the place of the next ritual killing. This waiting was making her anxious.

The door opened, and Anna walked inside. Today, she wore her usual black dress and an apron. Her light hair was braided into two neat plaits. She carried a small wicker basket filled with dried herbs. Jackie recognized eucalyptus and lavender.

Anna placed the basket on a table and checked the pot with melted wax. "Good job!"

"Thank you!" Jackie smiled. Even though she didn't make much progress in her investigation, at least candle-making was fun.

"Now, we need to put them into the forms," Anna said as she climbed a wooden stool and took four wooden cassettes, the forms for the future candles. She also brought several wicks.

Anna knew her job well – she showed Jackie how to grind the herbs using the pestle. Then she opened a wooden cassette containing the space for twelve candles. She attached the wick to the ends of the cylindrical pits to ensure it would be right in the middle of each candle. Then she closed the cassettes and poured some wax inside using a spoon. She sprinkled the dried eucalyptus inside and poured more wax.

Meanwhile, Jackie was dealing with the other cassette to prepare lavender candles. As she learned from Margaret, Divine Daughters sold these candles to the local stores as a remedy for cold, stress, and insomnia. Probably it was a good idea to keep one of the candles for herself. This mission was quite stressful, and she needed something to relax.

"So, I know who exactly went missing," Anna said out of the blue.

Jackie nearly dropped her spoon with hot wax. "What are you talking about?"

Anna gave her a sly look. "On the first night we talked, you said that you were looking for missing girls. Plural. So I checked my records carefully. And you know what? Carry wasn't the only one who disappeared after the conference with Claudia. There were others."

Jackie frowned and poured the leftovers of her wax into the cassette. Using this moment, she recollected her memories of that night – she was too tired, and she revealed more information than she was supposed to. Jackie did her best to correct herself, but it didn't work. And all this time, Anna was onto it!

"You don't need to explain anything to me," Anna lowered her voice. "I came to a conclusion on my own."

"Really?" Jackie asked. Her cassettes were full, and now she had nothing left but to listen to Anna's theories and try to persuade her to stay away from it.

Anna nodded enthusiastically. "I've been living here since August. So, I checked my diary and figured that since September, every month, one girl goes missing. It's always someone brand-new. I matched their characters, and I figured out that all of them had a strong sense of guilt that they buried deep inside. Also, they were obsessed with the idea that Claudia would take them on her trip, where they would have a chance to purify their soul." Anna paused, making sure that Jackie's full attention was on her. "Thus, I figured out who the criminal is. At first, I couldn't believe that Claudia could hurt them on purpose. But the more I thought of it, the more I realized that it made perfect sense. So tonight I went to her office pretending I was cleaning and found this." Anna took a small leather notebook out of her apron pocket and placed it on the table before Jackie.

Jackie opened it with her shaking fingers. The pictures of the five-beam stars, or pentagrams, were drawn in different places, and all the rest of the space was occupied with spells and descriptions of the rituals. Jackie raised her eyes at her. "Please, tell me she wouldn't start suspecting you stole it."

Anna gave her a surprised look. "Suspecting? Why don't you just use it to arrest her?"

Jackie took a deep breath, trying to calm her racing heart. Poor Anna had no idea what real evidence looked like, and now she put herself in grave danger. One thing was to teach her mental blocks so Claudia couldn't learn about their overnight talks, but bringing Anna into this investigation was a huge risk. "Okay, first, I'm not a guardian. I'm a lawyer, and I help the guardians who can make an arrest. And secondly, this notebook is only circumstantial evidence. It doesn't prove anything."

"But the girls went missing! Everything matches!"

"It's a well-built theory," Jackie agreed. "And you did a good job checking it. But it's only a theory. To catch a criminal, I need more – to hear a real threat or to catch her doing something illegal." She closed the notebook and gave it back to Anna. "Claudia is too dangerous, and now you put both of us at risk as she can use her Gift on you."

Anna didn't give up. "Fortunately, you taught me how to make a mental block."

"So what? If she finds out her diary is missing, she will suspect you! She might act with caution and not read you when you are conscious, but she can do it at night when you're asleep. Then, it will be too late for both of us!" Jackie paused to catch her breath. "The sooner you escape this place, the better."

"Escape?" Anna almost yelled. "I wasn't going to leave until –"

"You can't keep living here because she can easily read you!" Jackie interrupted. "If she figures out what you know, you may become the next victim."

Anna went silent, visibly upset with this reply.

"I can try to get my horse," Jackie started building a plan. "We will send you out tonight. I have people in the capital, and they can hide you in our shelter."

"What if I agree to become the next victim?" Anna suggested. "I can become bait."

Jackie breathed out heavily. It was the original plan – to have Anna as bait, so Jackie would follow her. But Anna was supposed to believe Claudia and be sincere. Now, considering what Anna was up to, it was too risky. "Absolutely not! She might not be able to read you, but mind readers can see insincerity. She will crack your plans right away!"

Anna didn't listen. "Let me help! I can talk to Claudia right after the ceremony and 'complain' about you. I can confess that I figured out your undercover mission and that her dirty secret might be in danger. Meanwhile, you will record our dialogue. Easy-peasy. She will be caught before she has a chance to find out about our plan!"

Jackie rolled her eyes, still unable to make any sense of this suicidal idea. "Still no. The risk is too high. She might get rid of both of us."

"Why are you scared?" Anna knitted her eyebrow. "The stakes were high from the beginning, and you knew that. And now, you just blow it when you have a chance?"

Jackie narrowed her eyes. Anna, a 16-year-old girl, now sat in front of her with her eyes glittering and her cheeks burning. Sometimes Elisa had the same look when talking about a new interesting investigation. Anna definitely had the passion of a true detective.

But she also was a rookie, and from her own experience, Jackie knew how reckless this attitude was. It might easily lead her to death, and Anna hardly realized it.

"Listen, I appreciate your desire to help. And if you want to solve crimes, I can write you a good recommendation letter to the Guardian Academy of Middle Lake. But please, for Divine's sake, don't get involved in this now. You are unprepared for such an operation, and you can ruin everything." Jackie pointed at the closed notebook. "If something goes wrong, the deaths of these four girls would be for nothing."

Anna shook her head in disappointment. Then she grabbed a notebook and stood up. "Fine. I'll place it back after lunchtime. She wouldn't notice it was missing."

Jackie nodded, relieved by this reply. "Good. And I'll try to arrange a horse ride for the girls before sunset to get you out of here."

"Maybe we can go for a ride tomorrow morning?" Anna suggested. "I just thought I organized a ceremony for you, so if I leave tonight, it would be too suspicious."

"And what if she reads you in the night?"

"She won't. We can take turns on night duty to ensure she won't enter our room with her key."

That made sense. Now, Jackie had hope that this frail plan would work. "Fine. But you'll leave first thing tomorrow."

"Of course." Anna smiled slyly and left the room.

Jackie looked around – her work here was done, and now she could focus on catching Claudia. Since Anna must be sent away, Jackie was the only candidate for the next ritual killing. Jackie had been playing her role well all this time, so there was no doubt that Claudia would invite her to make her next sacrifice. Then, she would be caught red-handed. It was better to act swiftly now. Tomorrow morning would be the perfect timing to talk to Claudia and suggest herself as a victim.

Jackie checked her apron and pulled out a Calling crystal. Before this move, she had to speak to Elisa and tell her about the plan change.

<h1 style="text-align:center">23</h1>

New Hope

"How are you?" Elisa asked, holding her Calling crystal. Now it shimmered with Jackie's blue Light – as clear as the ocean surface on a sunny day. She missed her to the point when her heart melted just because of listening to her voice.

"It's going alright," Jackie's voice replied from the crystal. "I'm really close to getting proof."

"Which proof? You said you read all the girls, and none of them knows a thing. We agreed that I must arrive there, so we will follow Claudia and Anna and prevent the next crime."

"Yes, it was an original plan," Jackie said apologetically. She spoke slowly, making Elisa anxious. "But there was a problem."

"Oh, dear... What happened?"

"Well, Anna got to know who I am."

Elisa's heart skipped a beat. This operation was a huge risk, and she would gladly get Jackie home without further delay. This waiting reminded her of that time three years ago when Jackie let the criminal gang kidnap her. It was too hard to go through the same experience again – knowing that her beloved one was in the enemy's nest. "Okay... How soon can you escape from there?"

Jackie exhaled into the crystal, creating noise. "It's alright. Anna knew about me from my first night here."

"What?" Elisa raised her voice. "She blew your cover, and you tell me just now? After two weeks?"

"Sorry, but I needed to gain her trust."

"What trust?!" Elisa had to take a deep breath not to shout. "It was the deal – you must stay safe."

"It's never really possible with this job," Jackie murmured. "Fortunately, it will be over soon. Tonight is the night when I have a ceremony to become The Daughter of Divine."

"I'll come," Elisa said.

"Please, don't," Jackie insisted. "Not until the morning. I plan to send Anna away right after breakfast, then face Claudia and suggest myself for her fake conference. I'm the only option, so she must agree. I'll record everything she says on my memory crystal, so we will have proof of her manipulations. I'll have to hide this proof in the house, so you'll need to collect it here."

"Jackie –"

"It will be alright," she interrupted. "Just warn the guardian team and follow us using the Searching spell."

"What about Anna? Are you sure she wouldn't give you away to Claudia?"

"Don't worry about that. Anna knows more than she should, but she is on our side. Since she learned about the killings, she started digging into it and found Claudia's notes on the ritual killings. She broke into her room and stole her diary."

"How reckless." Elisa shook her head. "And irresponsible. She could put you both in danger."

"I can't believe you are the one who says it," Jackie teased her.

Elisa stopped breathing at the painful memory. When she was in high school, she did exactly the same thing in a desperate trial to find a murderer who killed school girls in Triville. "This is why I say it. This mistake cost everyone too much."

"Now it's different," Jackie reassured her. "By the way, how was your part of our mission?"

"Quite well, actually. Julia agreed to join your healing program, and we got to Middle Lake together this morning."

"I'm so glad."

"Yes, that article that Laura gave me worked." Elisa exhaled loudly. "It wasn't smooth, and there were many tears, but eventually Julia agreed to try the therapy."

"It's never been easy. I think it's better if you stay with her tonight."

Elisa turned to the window. The thick layer of snow covered the main yard of the Guardian House, and now it was sparkling in the sun. The red dragon, Rose, played in the fresh snow with Edward, who said it would be useful to show people that dragons can be friendly and adorable creatures. Rose had already eaten her breakfast, and now they were running around the yard, Rose's tail sending white splashes into the air.

People started gathering around the fence to watch the real dragon. As it appeared, they were curious. With time, such interactions might create a good reputation for the dragon's farm.

"Elisa?" Jackie called her.

She sighed. "I miss you so much."

"Me too." Jackie's voice made goosebumps spread across her skin. "Promise that you come no earlier than at nine in the morning."

"Fine," Elisa said. "I'll get out of here at sunrise."

"Ok. I'll see you then."

"I can't wait." Elisa smiled as if Jackie could see her. "Please, be careful, dear."

"I will. I promise."

After she hung up, Elisa rose from her chair and took her coat hanging on the wall. She had come to work right after escorting Julia to the shelter, and now she couldn't think of anything else but Jackie, who had put herself in grave danger. Plus, as soon as Urchin figured out that Jackie was undercover, he constantly checked the news, triggering her exhausted nerves. She couldn't bear him anymore.

Jackie's advice to check on Julia seemed reasonable now – she didn't expect to hear much of her progress, but at least she could tell her that Rose was just alright and under watch here, in the Guardian House. Elisa put on her coat and left the room.

24

A Burnt Candle

The ceremony took place in a small room. The Daughters of Divine, clad in their white gowns adorned with sun embroidery on their sleeves and necklines, stood in a circle. Each of them, except Jackie, held a burning candle, casting dancing shadows across their focused faces.

Claudia entered the center of the circle and exchanged a serene glance with Jackie. "Today, we welcome a new Daughter of Divine into our circle. She will be your sister from this moment forward."

Jackie forced a smile and glanced at Anna, who stood within the circle with her eyes fixed on the floor, avoiding eye contact. This behavior was unsettling, especially considering that just before the ceremony, Jackie had bumped into Anna, who exited Claudia's office. Anna had refused to provide an explanation, citing her busy schedule with preparations. The worst thing was that Claudia was at her office at the time, indicating that they had likely discussed something, perhaps regarding the missing notebook.

Jackie gazed at the image of the sun adorning the wall, her lips moving silently in prayer. "Please, grant Anna the wisdom to steer clear of this mess and shield her from harm."

The flames from the candles flickered, casting reflections on the wall and causing the sun image to shimmer.

Claudia smiled warmly and raised her hand. "Let's welcome sister Jackie with our oath."

Jackie nodded, preparing herself for the ceremony. She had previously taken a guardian oath and now had to take this one. She was determined to do whatever it took to put an end to the injustice, as she had promised.

Claudia beckoned her forward, and Jackie stepped into the center of the circle. If it were up to her, Jackie would have arrested Claudia then and there. However, she knew she had to wait until the ceremony concluded. Thankfully, she had spoken to Elisa, asking her to arrive early in the morning. Jackie could only hope that Elisa's arrival wouldn't be too late.

If everything went according to plan, Jackie would speak with Anna after this awkward ceremony and unravel the events that transpired in Claudia's office. In the morning, she intended to confront Claudia alongside Elisa. The end was in sight.

As Claudia retreated, the girls began to move around Jackie, singing in harmony.

"All the worries dissolve tonight
In the radiance of your Light.
Let it shine from within,
Banish the darkness therein.

All shadows fade away
When you embrace this sacred way.

From this moment, forever entwined
You are the Daughter of Divine."

Jackie focused on the flickering flames of their candles, allowing their gentle glow to calm her nerves. She closed her eyes, basking in the soothing voices of her companions.

When the girls finished singing, Jackie opened her eyes to find Anna standing before her, holding a glass of red wine. The scent indicated it was a church-made spicy wine they had prepared themselves. They both knelt to the floor.

Anna met Jackie's gaze and offered a warm smile. "My dear sister, I present this wine to you as a token of welcome to our circle. From this moment on, our fates are intertwined, and I would sacrifice myself for you without hesitation."

Jackie harbored no doubts about Anna's sincerity – she was eager and too unpredictable. Jackie suspected that Anna would readily put herself in harm's way, and it was now Jackie's responsibility to safeguard her. Returning Anna's smile, Jackie recited the words she had prepared for the occasion. "Thank you, my dear sister. In accepting this gift from you, I pledge to watch over and defend you when needed. I vow to stand by your side through whatever trials may come."

Anna acknowledged her with a nod, her eyes shimmering in the candlelight. Jackie accepted the cup from Anna and took a sip. The wine was pleasantly warm, infused with hints of cinnamon and orange zest that made it exceptionally flavorful. Setting the cup down, Jackie battled a wave of dizziness. She typically refrained from alcohol consumption, indulging only on rare, momentous occasions. However, she now felt as though she had consumed an entire bottle. *This church booze is far too strong,* she noted to herself mentally.

Struggling to focus on Claudia's speech, Jackie took a deep breath. It seemed like her ability to listen was severely impaired. Anna remained seated before her, clutching her hands. If Jackie could read her thoughts, she would be able to uncover the truth. Yet, she was in no condition to do so. Her mind felt muddled, akin to mashed potatoes. Leaning in closer to inquire about the situation, Jackie was enveloped in a tight embrace from Anna, resting her head on Anna's shoulder.

Something isn't right, Jackie thought, as her limbs grew numb and her vision blurred. Anna drew nearer, her lips almost brushing against Jackie's ear as she whispered, "Under the mattress."

"What?" Jackie whispered back, her lips barely moving.

"Check under my mattress when you wake up. Do you understand?" Anna's urgent tone conveyed a sense of importance.

Jackie nodded faintly in response. Despite hearing Anna's words, she struggled to comprehend their meaning. Her tongue felt heavy and uncooperative, rendering her unable to speak. A sense of dread washed over her, fearing the possibility of succumbing to unconsciousness. *Was it poison?* If only she could inquire.

Anna offered a gentle pat on her head, providing reassurance. "Hush... everything will be alright."

Resolving to trust in Anna's pledge, Jackie closed her eyes, surrendering to the unknown.

25

❦

Perfect Bait

"What do you mean you can't wake her up?" Elisa almost shouted. It had been an hour since she arrived at the Daughters of Divine community, and now she was unable to revive Jackie.

Margaret, a young woman in charge, gave her a scared look. "We just can't. Last night she drank some wine, and it knocked her out. We were scared too, as it's never happened during the ceremony."

"What the hell did you give her? Where is the doctor?" Elisa bombarded her with questions.

Margaret offered her a glass of water, but Elisa waved her hand, refusing to drink anything in this place. Margaret placed the glass on the nightstand. "The village doctor arrived at midnight. He said it might be an allergic reaction as she had difficulty breathing. He left some herbs and said to give them to her when she wakes up. We need to wait."

Helpless, Elisa sat in a corner of Jackie's bed. She took her pale hand in hers, checking for a pulse repeatedly. It was calm, as if nothing had happened. The issue was that Jackie was in a deep slumber, and no one could wake her up. As far as Elisa knew, Jackie wasn't allergic to anything, indicating that it was a potion that had affected her in this way. *If only I didn't listen to her and arrived earlier!*

Elisa buried her head in her hands, trying to calm herself. Even if Jackie had been poisoned, it could be a strong sedative that would wear off with time or a slow-acting poison for which they might need to find an antidote. She didn't trust the village doctor, but fortunately, she had her own expert. She touched her Calling crystal and thought of Edward.

"Yes?" His groggy voice emanated from the crystal, causing Margaret to startle. Elisa couldn't help but snicker. Well, she deserved it.

"Hi, Ed!" Elisa greeted him. "Listen, how can we determine if a person has been poisoned?"

"Let me think," he said. A long pause followed. Elisa wasn't sure if he had just woken up or was contemplating how to explain it to her, as she was never particularly adept in chemistry. Perhaps both. "Do you have someone to assist you?"

"Sort of," Elisa replied, giving Margaret a meaningful look, prompting her to come closer.

"What do I need to do?" Margaret asked, ready to help, her hands resting on the pocket of her white apron.

Edward's voice took on a cheerful tone. "I hear a very lovely voice. What's your name?"

"Margaret," she said with a shy smile, unaware that Edward couldn't see her. "And what about you, magic crystal?"

He chuckled. "Actually, I'm a real human, and my name is Edward. I simply communicate through this crystal. By the way, I invented this method of communication."

"Alright, we understand," Elisa hurried Edward along before he veered off track. "So, inventor Edward, someone gave Jackie church wine, and now we can't wake her up."

"Oh, that's not good," he remarked.

"I know that. The question is – what should we do?"

"Look, if you can find the wine, we can analyze it using different ingredients. Some poisons react in a specific manner when mixed with herbs –"

"Sorry, Edward," Margaret interjected. "I've already washed the cup. And the doctor mentioned she was allergic."

"You called for a doctor? Very good," Edward commended.

Margaret blushed at the unexpected praise.

Elisa let out a weary sigh. "Please, Ed, tell me what to do. Then you two can chat as much as you want."

"Sorry," Edward said. "I meant that an allergic reaction is a valuable clue. Some herbs can indeed cause it, like mugwort. Someone could have added it to the wine."

"So, what should I do now?"

"It should have a temporary effect, but you can expedite the detox process by giving her mint and lemon water. Although she is currently asleep, you can burn the mint near her head so she can smell it and awaken," Edward advised.

"Alright, I'll call you later," Elisa said before ending the call.

Margaret fetched a mint twig, and Elisa snapped her fingers to ignite the electric sparkles. The twig began to smolder slowly, filling the room with smoke.

"Is it working?" Margaret inquired.

"I have no idea," Elisa replied, moving the twig over Jackie's head. Tears welled up in her eyes. "Please, wake up, dear. I need you now."

Margaret regarded her with suspicion before placing a comforting hand on her shoulder. "You are in love with her, aren't you?"

Elisa nodded silently.

"Well, in that case," Margaret began, lowering her gaze. "I once read that a kiss might work."

Elisa gave her a puzzled look. "What are you talking about?"

Margaret shrugged. "If there was a toxin, the doctor would have detected it. He checked everything, and I observed him. But what if she wasn't poisoned or allergic? Then someone might have cast a spell on her."

"A Sleeping spell?" Elisa blinked. She had read about it in an old fairy tale but had never witnessed it in action. Perhaps because it was a method of revenge from a forgotten past, favored by women. Modern criminals tended to prefer more direct methods – poisons, knives, fireballs.

Margaret nodded. "I'm so sorry, but another girl, Anna, was with her last night. She possesses a Persuading Gift. I never imagined she could harm someone. Until now."

"Where is she now?"

"Gone," Margaret replied in a hushed tone. "Claudia and she departed early at sunrise. I believe Claudia may have suspected Anna and attempted to bring her to the guardians."

Elisa shook her head. If Mrs. Turner had appeared at a Guardian House, Urchin would have informed Elisa immediately. Or Walter. No, the women had simply left, and based on their conversation with Jackie the previous day, this girl, Anna, was in grave danger.

Elisa gazed at Jackie's serene face, her eyes closed and her rosy lips slightly parted. She appeared beautiful in her deep slumber, but it was time for her to awaken.

Leaning in close, Elisa kissed her gently on the lips before pulling back, waiting anxiously. Margaret remained silent, observing the scene.

Jackie began to breathe deeply, then slowly opened her emerald eyes and sat up, looking at them in astonishment. "Hey."

"Oh, dear." Elisa embraced Jackie, ensuring she wouldn't faint again. Jackie still seemed slightly dizzy, but overall, she appeared to be okay.

"What happened?" Jackie inquired after finishing her glass of lemon water.

Margaret sighed. "It was Anna. She enchanted you last night."

"Like a sleeping beauty," Elisa remarked. "Did you know about her Gift?"

Jackie's eyes widened as she processed the information. Then, she slapped her forehead. "Oh, shoot!" Jackie sprang to her feet and hurried to the opposite bed. She removed the pillow and dropped it to the floor before shifting the mattress.

Underneath, there was a leather diary and a blinking memory crystal.

"Oh, silly. What have you done?" Jackie whispered, her hands clutching her messy charcoal hair.

Margaret walked over to comfort her, while Elisa moved to the bed to examine the evidence left by Anna.

Elisa opened the diary, and an envelope fell out. *"For Jackie,"* it read in neat handwriting. *"To open when you finally wake up."* Elisa frowned. It was a rookie mistake – she had no way of knowing when Jackie would awaken. Anna had left no clue for Elisa. If Jackie remained asleep for an extended period, she could potentially die from exhaustion or dehydration. By then, Anna would likely be dead, sacrificed in a soul-summoning ritual. Elisa blinked.

Unless that was the plan all along. Anna's death would break the spell, and Jackie would be safe. Did Anna sacrifice herself?

Elisa opened the envelope and gave them a curious look. Jackie glanced at Margaret and gestured for her to read it. Elisa nodded and began to read the letter aloud.

"Dear sister Jackie,

I am deeply sorry that I had to depart in this manner. Perhaps every-one believes you experienced an extended dream, but the reality is that it was me all along. I am the member of the cult you were seeking. By the time you read this, I will have departed, joining the eternal Divine Light.

I never intended to cause you harm, and I understand that you have many unanswered questions, so I will reveal everything now. Initially, Claudia harbored suspicions about you from the moment you arrived, cautioning me not to engage with you. While you were half-asleep, I used my Persuasive Gift on you, prompting you to divulge the truth about your investigation. Subsequently, I erased this portion of our interaction from your memory, leading you to believe you were unable to fall asleep.

Upon learning about your mission, I descended to draft a compre-hensive report on you, which I was to deliver to Claudia. However, you awoke and disrupted my efforts."

Elisa paused, absorbing the contents of the letter before continu-ing.

"Remember our pleasant conversation by the fireplace? I now feel im-mense regret for deceiving you. However, it was my duty to check on you. I hope that one day you can find it in your heart to forgive me.

That evening, I mentioned making personal records in my Diary, but I failed to disclose that for months, I resided under this roof with the pur-

pose of spying on the new girls Claudia brought in. I believed I was acting for a noble cause – witnessing their anguish and desperation to alleviate their suffering. They willingly agreed to sacrifice themselves, as Claudia assured them it was the sole method to save another life. I viewed it as a great honor. I assisted Claudia in achieving this honor for myself – to become the fifth soul. However, after completing my assignment, I encountered you, and you instilled doubt within me.

After that night, you began training me to create mental blocks, but it was more than that. You taught me the essence of freeing my mind. We conversed frequently, and every word you spoke illuminated the truth – that these girls were innocent victims of manipulation. They agreed to sacrifice themselves because they lacked knowledge of alternative methods to cope with their pain. It took time before I acknowledged that I, too, fell into the same category. I harbored my own pain, yet I believed I was beyond redemption. I perceived myself as flawed – possessing a manipulative Gift that I utilized to deceive those around me, coupled with actions in my past that I felt ashamed of.

Throughout my life, I perpetuated lies out of fear, concealing my true self from others. I did so because I was unaware of any other approach. I deemed myself too feeble to embrace honesty like others, to simply be a flawed human capable of making mistakes. I deceived my teachers in school to secure good grades and misled my friends to project a more favorable image of myself.

I didn't fabricate my escape from the arranged marriage. That was the truth. However, I never formulated grand aspirations for my future. Truthfully, I harbored self-loathing and ventured to Middle Lake due to its notorious criminal reputation. My parents cautioned me about the dangers, unaware that death was my sole desire.

As I neared Middle Lake, I encountered Claudia, the only individual impervious to my unique Gift. Presumably, she had mastered the art of blocking external influences. She extended an invitation to join the com-

munity, and we deliberated on the planned sacrifices. At that juncture, death seemed the sole path to liberation.

Claudia served not only as my mentor but as the first person who refrained from passing judgment on the aspects I had suppressed – my anguish and my deceitful tendencies. Despite being privy to all my secrets, she never held me in contempt. In her presence, even I began to harbor less disdain for myself. Prior to meeting her, I harbored a profound fear of shedding my facade, oblivious to the burden it imposed. Everything transformed upon meeting her, the sole individual who illuminated a path to liberation from it.

Subsequently, I crossed paths with you, Jackie, and you upended my world. You shared your narrative and emphasized the importance of self-forgiveness and living authentically. You urged me not to succumb to manipulation fueled by fear, but rather to embrace my true self and strive for personal growth through honesty, not for the sake of others, but for myself.

Your words resonated with sincerity. You possess a fearlessness in embracing your true self, Jackie. You professed forgiveness, and I believed you. I am confident that you will extend forgiveness once more upon learning my truth."

Elisa's eyes filled with tears as she processed Anna's final words.

"But forgiveness won't be enough. Now, aware of what I did as Claudia's puppet, I can't put you or anyone else in danger. So I decided to sacrifice myself. Today, I won't do it to get rid of my pain. Honestly, I never felt so good for a long time as now my life has a real purpose. All I want now is to give you a chance to catch Claudia. She thinks that I poisoned you because she ordered me to do it, but I only charmed you with a Sleeping spell.

Now I'm gone, but you are alive. So live your life wisely. Just before the ceremony, I recorded our talk with Claudia, discussing the ritual. I hope it will be enough to put her in prison and stop this heartless manipulation. Claudia must be somewhere on her way back from my village now. So catch her and arrest her. You have my blessing.

Sincerely,
Anna.

P.S. I hope that you will tell everything to Margaret. She will be in full charge now and can do so much good. And I know that she will do it sincerely, from all her big heart."

Elisa lowered the letter and rubbed her forehead. Jackie was still in shock, and Margaret stood over her, her eyes brimming with tears. She wiped them with the corner of her apron.

"I'm so sorry about Anna. She was such a good soul," Margaret said softly.

Elisa stood up, a determined look in her eyes. "Don't mourn her before she is dead. Anna believed that Jackie would awaken immediately after her sacrifice, but it didn't happen that way."

Jackie's eyes widened with hope. "Are you saying there's still a chance to save her?"

"Absolutely," Elisa affirmed. "We just need her belongings to perform a Searching spell. We will find her."

"Thank you, Divine!" Margaret exclaimed, raising her hands to the ceiling. "I need her here. Please, bring her home."

"I will," Jackie assured her. "I promise."

26

Fate Roulette

Rose floated gracefully below the pinkish clouds, savoring the fresh wind. Elisa gripped the reins tightly, peering over the dragon's ears. Anna's brooch, now aglow with the blue light of the Searching spell, hovered before them. Elisa secured it with a rope connected to the saddle, allowing her to discern the direction in which to fly.

Jackie embraced her from behind, causing Elisa to catch her breath as she absorbed the beauty of the moment. Despite the chaos of their vacation-turned-investigation, they remained united. Elisa was relieved that it was nearing its end. She gently pulled on the reins, slowing the dragon to lessen the force of the wind against her face. Turning to Jackie, she said, "Once I apprehend Claudia, we'll wait for Theo. He should arrive in two hours to escort her to the Guardian House of Triville. After that, I plan to abandon all work and retreat to our home, where we can focus on caring for each other."

"That sounds absolutely perfect," Jackie murmured, her smile lighting up her face before she leaned in for a lingering, passionate kiss.

Elisa savored the sweetness and warmth of Jackie's lips, losing herself in the moment as time seemed to stand still, leaving just the two of them suspended in the tranquil evening sky. The only sounds were the gentle whisper of the wind and the steady beat of their hearts, creating a soothing rhythm in the silence. The sun cast a warm glow over them as it dipped below the horizon, bathing their entwined bodies in its golden light.

"Almost there," Jackie whispered, glancing over her shoulder.

Elisa reluctantly turned her gaze forward, feeling a pang of disappointment as the blue light surrounding the brooch began to flicker, signaling their imminent arrival. The fleeting moment of intimacy was over. With a heavy heart, Elisa tugged on the reins, guiding Rose downward in a slow descent towards the ground below.

Surveying the landscape, they found themselves in a remote, snow-covered expanse, surrounded by towering mountain peaks and a valley stretching out beneath them. They were nearing the High Canyons, a location that was quite expected given the proximity of Anna's home village.

Elisa could only hope that they would locate Claudia soon and bring her to justice. The evidence contained in the recording that Anna had entrusted to the memory crystal was damning enough to ensure a lengthy prison sentence for her.

As Rose touched down at the base of the hill, taking a few slow, deliberate steps to come to a complete stop, Elisa praised her, patting her head affectionately. Rose wagged her tail enthusiastically, inadvertently crushing some small rocks nearby.

"Easy, girl!" Elisa chuckled, trying to calm the excited dragon.

Jackie dismounted and landed gracefully on the ground, with Elisa following suit. From their vantage point, they could make out the dark silhouettes of the mountains, illuminated by the flickering light of a fire burning in one of the nearby caves. It appeared to be a short distance away, perhaps a mere ten-minute walk.

Jackie placed a reassuring hand on Elisa's shoulder. "Ready?"

"Always," Elisa affirmed with a determined nod. "It's a perfect night to save a life."

As they approached the cave, the sky had darkened, with the first stars beginning to twinkle above, partially obscured by wispy clouds. A luminous full moon hung low in the sky, casting an eerie glow over the mountains. The sounds emanating from the cave were muffled, but the distinct voices of women could be heard. Sensing a foreboding presence, Elisa slowed her pace.

"What's wrong?" Jackie asked.

"I'm not sure," Elisa replied, her voice tinged with uncertainty. "I just have a bad feeling."

"We could wait for Theo."

Elisa shook her head. "We're running out of time. Just... stay behind me, okay? I'll take the lead, and you can be prepared to intervene if Mrs. Turner attempts to flee. Have your Paralyzing spell at the ready."

Jackie raised her hand, conjuring a shimmering silver ball of Paralyzing energy in her palm. "Let's go."

Elisa entered the cave cautiously, her hand poised to unleash her Gift at a moment's notice. Inside, as she had anticipated, two women sat on the stone floor on opposite sides of a crackling fire. A chalk circle was drawn around each of them, adding to the air of mystique and tension in the dimly lit cavern.

Elisa raised her hand, releasing violet sparks of electricity. "Hands up so I can see them!" she commanded.

The two women turned towards her. The younger one appeared to be Anna, while the older woman was Mrs. Turner, a familiar figure from Elisa's childhood.

"Mrs. Turner! It's been a while," Elisa greeted her.

Mrs. Turner furrowed her brow. "Elisa?! What brings you here?"

"In the name of the King, you are under arrest," Elisa declared. "Stand up and move to the wall, showing me both of your hands."

Mrs. Turner chuckled, glancing at Anna. "She said move. You're free to go."

Anna shook her head resolutely. "I'm not giving up that easily."

Jackie, who had been concealed behind the wall, emerged and approached the fire in the center of the cave. "Anna, please. There's no need for this. I have all the evidence necessary to make an arrest."

Anna's eyebrows shot up in surprise. "You?"

"Yes, me. I'm here and ready to help," Jackie affirmed. "You can trust me now."

"I can't," Anna replied, her expression filled with concern as she glanced back at Mrs. Turner. "If I step out of the circle first, she will perish. The same goes for her. We must remain seated until the fire burns out, and then the flames will determine our fate."

Elisa lowered her hand, realizing the gravity of the situation. These chalk circles held a sinister purpose. It was a twisted mind game where the loser faced death. "Remove these spells now!" Elisa demanded, looking Mrs. Turner in the eye.

Mrs. Turner's laughter reverberated through the cavern, echoing off the high ceiling. "Oh, Elisa. I always knew you would grow into someone extraordinary. You were always too nosy. In my time, girls like you were deemed hopeless."

"Thankfully, it's no longer 'your time,'" Elisa retorted.

"I know," Mrs. Turner conceded with a nod. "So, Anna, you're free to depart whenever you wish, and I will make the ultimate sacrifice."

Elisa reached into her inner pocket and produced the star-shaped amulet she had confiscated from Julia. "No more sacrifices," she declared, fixing Mrs. Turner with a steely gaze. "We are aware of your intentions regarding your grandchild and how you deceived Julia."

"Did you steal that?" Mrs. Turner inquired, her expression clouded with annoyance. "Regardless, return it to Julia once this is resolved."

"No. Julia entrusted this to me to prevent you from perpetuating these senseless killings."

"Senseless?" Mrs. Turner sneered. "Your interference renders their deaths meaningless!"

Out of the corner of her eye, Elisa observed Jackie's movements. Jackie positioned herself behind Mrs. Turner, poised to unleash a Paralyzing spell if necessary. *Well done*, Elisa thought. With Jackie's support, they could at least prevent Mrs. Turner from making any sudden or dangerous moves.

"Is that why you murdered those girls?" Jackie interjected. "Were you under the impression that you were helping Julia?"

"I'm not a murderer," Mrs. Turner said dismissively. "I merely granted them a favor. These girls were burdened with guilt. They pleaded with me to end their lives once I proposed the ritual!"

"Why did you introduce such ideas to them in the first place?" Jackie persisted. "You were aware of their vulnerability. They were inexperienced, lost souls in need of guidance. Your role was to mentor them, to help them navigate and heal their emotional wounds!"

"It was Divine's guidance," Mrs. Turner explained. "Many years ago, I collaborated with a priest from Triville, and together, we were entrusted with safeguarding the Forbidden Manuscript. Within its pages lay a ritual for soul attraction, which I read out of sheer curiosity. I had no intention of ever utilizing it, and truthfully, I had largely forgotten about the spell. However, upon learning of Julia's plight through a letter from the same Triville priest, I journeyed to Triville. We discussed the matter, and to my surprise, he possessed the same amulet that he kept in his safe. Naturally, I borrowed it."

"You mean you stole it," Elisa corrected her. "What became of that priest?"

Mrs. Turner shrugged. "I heard he was unable to cope with his guilt over losing the amulet and subsequently resigned."

"How considerate of you," Elisa remarked sarcastically.

"I was devastated," Mrs. Turner retorted, casting Elisa a disdainful glance. "You are aware of the hardships our family has endured."

A wave of sadness washed over Elisa. Among all her friends and acquaintances, only Kyle's parents could rival the level of pain and tragedy that her own family had endured. But despite the hardships they faced, it did not justify Mrs. Turner's actions in taking innocent lives. Unlike Julia, who struggled to come to terms with her loss, Mrs. Turner, being older and more experienced, should have known better and handled her grief in a more constructive manner.

"When I first met Anna," Mrs. Turner continued, "I was overwhelmed by my sorrow and broke down in front of her. She offered to assist me on this path –"

"Did you realize that it involved dark magic?" Jackie interjected, her tone laced with accusation.

Anna, now prompted to speak, lowered her gaze. "I'm sorry. I only intended to sacrifice myself. I never meant for so much harm to come from it."

Jackie shook her head in disbelief. "Claudia, you were a senior priest! How could you not have been aware of the consequences that such rituals have for both newborn children and their mothers?"

Mrs. Turner adjusted a lock of hair behind her ear. "I delved deeply into that research. The individuals involved in that scientific experiment were elderly and grappling with terminal illnesses. Their willingness to sacrifice themselves stemmed from a place of despair. I believe this is why the ritual failed – the children whose souls were summoned to their mothers inherited similar afflictions. Consider this: the participants were already unwell and sought an escape from their suffering. Consequently, they drew spirits bearing the same burdens, perpetuating a cycle of anguish. The repercussions were fivefold, intensifying the suffering and shortening their lives."

"It means that humans cannot tamper with the cycle of life and death," Jackie explaied for all present. "This principle is outlined in a sacred text of Divine. One cannot evade their destiny – when faced with a challenge, it must be confronted, as these trials are meant to enrich our minds and fortify our spirits."

"Exactly," Elisa said. "And what about the young women who were sacrificed? Did you consider the potential impact on your grandchild? Would they inherit and endure those traumas, amplified fivefold?"

"I contemplated it thoroughly," Mrs. Turner explained, gesturing with a touch of inappropriate elegance. "The crux of the matter lay in ensuring the girls embraced their fate willingly. If they approached their sacrifice with genuine selflessness, devoid of personal desires, the ritual would have unfolded flawlessly."

Elisa let out a heavy sigh. Mrs. Turner possessed a compelling way with words, but the problem lay in the fact that most people only thought of personal gain. While the four victims had indeed sacrificed their lives while young and healthy, they had done so solely to escape their anguish. What a tragic outcome! Like many other young women of their tender age, they were unaware of alternative methods of healing.

"How can you be certain of the sincerity of their sacrifice?" Jackie inquired.

Mrs. Turner shrugged nonchalantly. "What can I say? I did not physically end their lives. I merely conducted the ritual and left their fate to chance."

"Fate?" Jackie and Elisa asked together.

She nodded. "You see, I told Anna that the person who leaves the circle first will survive. But in certain cases, the spell would work just the opposite, and you can die as soon as you leave the circle. If your actions are sincere and you are ready to give your life away to let someone live, then the Light will take you, and your soul will be free and clear. But if you are afraid and you leave it wishing someone bad out of your fear or anger... Well, then, the Light will take *my* soul."

Anna's eyes filled with sorrow as she looked at Mrs. Turner. "I should never have agreed to this. I thought I would be the one to die, and they would apprehend you. I don't want you to perish."

"Are you angry with me, my daughter?" Mrs. Turner inquired.

Anna nodded, a tear tracing a path down her cheek. "Please forgive me, Mother. I believed you had taken their lives, but they had a choice."

Mrs. Turner smiled gently. "I forgive you. You did not poison Jackie as you claimed. This proves that you possess goodness within you. Do not fret. Trust in your fate and depart."

Anna rose to her feet, ready to exit the chalk circle.

"Hold on!" Elisa interjected. She couldn't fathom that Mrs. Turner was genuinely willing to risk her own life. Most likely, she just manipulated Anna. Now, she was waiting for Anna to take a step, so the final victim would spare her life. "I have a question."

Mrs. Turner fluttered her eyelashes. "Sure. I can respond if I'm still among the living."

"How did the other girls meet their end? Did they all leave the circle first?"

"Yes."

Elisa's suspicions were confirmed. There was no intricate spell at play – only the confusion that Mrs. Turner had orchestrated. This confusion had instilled unnecessary fear and anxiety in the victims, leading them to succumb to their fears and exit the chalk circle first. If all four victims had left their circles first and perished, it indicated that the chalk had served as a protective barrier against the supposed spell of fire. To test her theory, Elisa could try to lure Mrs. Turner out of her place.

"What if *you* stand up and take that step?" Elisa proposed.

Mrs. Turner stood up and adjusted her dress. "Why not? We can try it this way, too."

"No!" Anna cried out. "Don't do it!"

"Let's all take a moment to calm down," Jackie interjected. "Where is the text of this spell? I can read it to verify your claims, ensuring Anna's safety."

"It's in my notebook," Mrs. Turner replied. "In my travel bag."

"I've read that notebook, and it checks out," Anna confirmed. "I am willing to try. If it is my fate to perish, then so be it. In any case, Claudia will be apprehended. However, if my life holds promise and a significant purpose, then I will remain –"

"And I will depart," Mrs. Turner concluded.

Elisa shook her head in fruistration. Perhaps she needed to be direct in order to achieve her goal. "Okay, okay, I got it. Mrs. Turner is very thoughtful and tricked everyone into this mind game. But the truth is that this chalk circle is only protection. There is no such complex spell and it never was. The one who leaves the circle first will die. That's it. But to make people believe her, she faked this spell in her notebook, just in case Anna or anyone else would read it. And it worked just brilliantly!"

A grin spread across Mrs. Turner's face, and Elisa caught a fleeting shadow in her eyes – a look of enjoyment and control, reminiscent of bullies reveling in their power over their victims. Everything was a game to Mrs. Turner, and she held all the cards – manipulating their fears, worries, and lives with ease. Elisa recognized this behavior all too well, having once been a bully herself. But she doubted Mrs. Turner would ever change.

Mrs. Turner cleared her throat and lifted the hem of her dress, poised to take that fateful step. "Fine, if no one believes me, I'll do it!"

"NO!" Anna's eyes widened, poised to cross the chalk line.

Elisa jumped to Anna, preventing her from leaving the circle. She stepped into the circle herself and enveloped Anna from behind, clasping her hands tightly to prevent her from taking a step.

"Let me go!" Anna screamed, struggling against Elisa's grasp.

Elisa hushed her and shot Mrs. Turner a challenging look. If Mrs. Turner wanted to play games, then let it be a battle between the two of them. "Go on, Mrs. Turner, demonstrate how much you truly care for your 'Divine Daughter'!"

Mrs. Turner's demeanor shifted – her eyes narrowed, her breaths grew labored. Though she remained motionless, she visibly strained against an invisible force. "What have you done? Now, if I step out of my circle, both of you may face dire consequences. Release Anna. She has already made her choice."

Jackie gasped, her hands releasing the spell, which shattered into shimmering silver fragments on the stone floor. "Why?"

Mrs. Turner turned to Jackie. "Why what?"

"Why are you placing this burden on *her*?" Jackie shook her head in disdain. "It's not a true choice if you leave her with no alternative but to bear the weight of someone's death. Naturally, Anna doesn't wish your death. She is a kind-hearted person who would sacrifice herself, leaving trash like you to roam this earth."

Mrs. Turner cocked her head and chuckled, causing Anna to cease her struggles in Elisa's grasp. "Sharp observation!" Mrs. Turner remarked, her irritation no longer concealed. "In case you haven't grasped it yet, the entire system is rotten. This is why good people perish, while cunning ones reign supreme."

"We must strive to change it," Jackie stated. "My condolences for the loss of your daughter, and I mean your biological daughter, Rebecca Turner."

"You've learned her name. How delightful!" Mrs. Turner retorted sarcastically.

"There is no need for pretense. It wasn't Julia's child's death that propelled you down this path. It began long ago, with the death of your daughter, Rebecca."

Mrs. Turner remained silent, her jaw clenched, as she locked eyes with Jackie. Elisa held her breath, witnessing how effortlessly Jackie had uncovered the underlying cause of Mrs. Turner's actions.

"Yes, it all began with her death," Mrs. Turner confessed. "I attempted to forgive those responsible for her demise, but I could never bring myself to do so."

"It would have been an impossible task to ask of you."

"I simply needed someone to lean on! I was a priest, and when I was at my lowest, they cast me out of the church! I didn't put up a fight. Instead, I walked away and established my own community. I prayed daily for my son's happiness. At least he had his wonderful, loving wife by his side. And look at what befell them."

"I understand," Jackie responded with a nod, offering Mrs. Turner a moment of empathy and understanding. "I am deeply sorry for the pain you have endured, and I understand that there are no words that can ease your suffering. The loss of Rebecca was a tragedy, and it is unjust that she met such a fate. However, her story sparked a transformation in our society. Her legacy has brought about significant changes, and we continue to strive for progress each day. But if you persist in manipulating these girls, leading them down the same path, this cycle of cruelty will persist. The cycle of suffering will perpetuate, causing women like yourself to endure repeated anguish. Please, release this spell and let us engage in dialogue."

Mrs. Turner turned her gaze towards Anna. "Too late for that. This spell is intertwined with our blood, and we must make choices until the flame extinguishes. With the final sparkle, the future will be determined."

Elisa let out a heavy sigh. Jackie's impassioned plea had been powerful, but Mrs. Turner remained unmoved. Regretfully, she was beyond help. Elisa's gaze shifted to the flickering flames. *Is Mrs. Turner bluffing again, trying to buy more time?* They still had time to resolve this, but the tension in the room was escalating with each passing moment.

"Okay, just push her," Mrs. Turner instructed Elisa.

Elisa blinked in disbelief. "What?"

Mrs. Turner's smile twisted into a malevolent grin. "You were correct about the spell. Once you step into a protective circle, the spell marks you, causing the death of the first person who exits it. So push Anna. After all, she is a lost cause. Too pure for this cruel world."

Anna gasped, her eyes wide with shock as she looked back at Elisa. "It's okay, let me go. You've heard enough to have her arrested."

Jackie moved closer to Mrs. Turner, her voice firm. "You do realize that I can push you as well, don't you?"

Mrs. Turner let out a laugh. "You would never have the courage to do it. It takes true bravery to take a life."

Jackie rubbed her temples wearily. "Okay. I need a moment to collect my thoughts." With a wink at Elisa, she turned and exited the cave, leaving only the three of them behind. The crackling of the fire and the pounding of their hearts filled the tense silence.

Elisa was initially puzzled by the situation until she heard the unmistakable roar of a dragon – Rose. She held Anna close, whispering urgently, "Trust me, and don't move."

Anna nodded in agreement.

The heavy thuds of the dragon's landing reverberated through the cave, accompanied by another deafening roar. Mrs. Turner's expression shifted to one of fear. "Run!"

"Is that a wild dragon?!" Elisa mustered wide-eyed terror.

Anna's fear was genuine, evident in her trembling form. "There's no escaping them!"

Mrs. Turner glanced towards the dark cave exit, where the dragon drew closer.

"Do you know what happens when you disturb their habitat?" Elisa asked, her voice quivering with feigned fear. She was proving to be quite an adept actress. "They tear you apart with their razor-sharp claws. And they are impervious to magic."

"What should I do?" Mrs. Turner asked, her hands clutching her dress in fear.

"Remove the spell," Elisa suggested.

"I can't," Mrs. Turner replied, meeting Anna's gaze. "It's a blood-based spell and cannot be undone. Truly." With a resigned sigh, she stepped back, remaining within her chalk circle. Her body tensed, poised to leap forward and push Anna and Elisa from their positions.

She won't win this time, Elisa thought.

Time seemed to slow as she focused on Mrs. Turner, anticipating her move. The fire crackled fiercely. The dragon's roar echoed closer to the cave entrance, prompting Mrs. Turner to spring forward like a predator ready to strike.

Without hesitation, Elisa thrust her hand forward, palm open. A bolt of lightning surged from her fingertips, striking Mrs. Turner mid-air and hurling her against the cave wall. Mrs. Turner collided with the stone surface and crumpled to the ground like a discarded puppet.

Elisa relaxed her grip, allowing Anna to slip from her embrace.

Ignoring the looming danger, Anna rushed to Mrs. Turner's side. Suddenly, the fire coalesced into a blazing sphere above them and shot towards their direction. In an instant, darkness enveloped them, accompanied by an eerie silence.

"What just happened?" Elisa's voice cut through the darkness.

The only response was the sound of quiet sobs. *At least one of them was still alive, but who?*

Jackie emerged from the cave entrance, casting a soft blue Light that illuminated her apprehensive expression. Elisa's gaze shifted to the wall where the deadly flame had originated. Mrs. Turner lay on the ground, her chest bearing a circular burn mark. Her arms lay limply at her sides, her once vibrant blue eyes now lifeless and wide open.

Anna shook Mrs. Turner's shoulders, attempting to rouse her, but it was futile. With a solemn touch, Anna closed Mrs. Turner's eyes, bidding her a final farewell.

Elisa let out a heavy sigh. Humans were prone to deceit and often acted out of self-interest. However, at least this particular ordeal was now resolved, and they had managed to save Anna. Anna had shown bravery and possessed good morals. With the right guidance and practice, she had the potential to become a formidable guardian.

Jackie moved closer to Anna, offering a comforting pat on her shoulder. "Claudia is now at peace."

"She deceived me and everyone else," Anna said, her eyes brimming with tears. "But why do I feel such sorrow then?"

"Perhaps she did deceive you, but she was also a human, one who was deeply wounded," Jackie explained, her voice tinged with empathy. "I wish I could have helped Claudia. She was broken and in need of healing, not punishment."

"Could she truly be healed?"

Jackie shrugged. "She could have tried. Unfortunately, she didn't seize that opportunity. Now, all you can do is try to forgive her, so that her spirit may find solace in her next journey."

Anna tenderly stroked Mrs. Turner's hair. "Of course, I forgive you." She raised her eyes at jackie. "What was all that commotion? I really thought it was a dragon."

Jackie offered a sad smile. "That was Rose. She's the dragon belonging to our dear friends. She's quite friendly. I only had her roar to prompt Claudia to release the trap. I never anticipated it would end up like this."

Elisa slid her frozen hands into her pockets and felt something sharp – a pendant. She retrieved it, revealing all five points of the star gleaming brightly. "How do we properly dispose of this?"

Jackie had a suggestion at the ready. "We shouldn't let any woman wear it on her chest. We must take it to a secure location."

"Like a laboratory?" Elisa pondered, considering Edward's expertise in handling such dangerous artifacts.

"Let's just place it in a secure bag for now," Jackie proposed. "Our priority is to transport Claudia to Triville, and we can address the amulet later."

"Agreed."

Outside the cave, Rose awaited near the entrance. Elisa carefully stowed the amulet in a secure pocket of her road bag, which was fastened to the saddle. She affectionately patted the dragon's head. "Well done, Rose. You performed admirably today in your brother's absence."

Rose emitted a contented purr in acknowledgment.

In the darkened sky, the sound of powerful wings flapping drew closer. Elisa lifted her gaze, observing Rei as he descended and landed near the caves.

Part 3

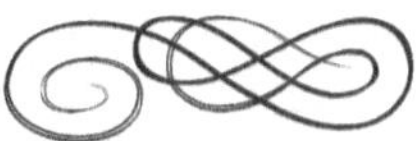

The Wind of Change

27

Long Lost Trace

The amulet bounced in her hand. Elisa moved to the window to inspect it closer. Even though it was a bright spring day, the crystals had lost their inner shine. Now, they looked like shards of glass.

"How did it happen?" She turned to Edward. "You said it was here all the time."

He shrugged. "I never let anyone walk in my lab besides several guardians. Plus, when I ran some tests last night, it was just fine."

"Which tests?" Elisa placed the amulet on the desk. Edward's workplace was tidy and neat, and it was hard to accuse him of sloppiness.

The amulet they delivered to Middle Lake Guardian House went directly to Edward. He quickly figured out that the amulet wasn't a trap for the souls, and it brought everyone relief. As he explained, it was just a magnet – the girls who died in that ritual left a reflection of their Light in the crystal.

It took five sacrifices to gather enough energy to open a 'spiritual portal,' as Edward called it. This portal was attracting a new spirit, shining like a star in the dark space, calling the soul to be reborn as a human in this world. The amulet only worked with women who wore it on their chest, resonating with their heartbeat.

For months after Elisa had brought it, the amulet remained untouched by any human, continuing to shine brightly. However, this morning, it seemed to have lost its luster.

"I tried to understand how this magnet works. I wanted to find a way to attract the spirits without resorting to black magic," Edward explained, touching the crystals with his fingertips. "Silly me. It probably just got recharged because I ran too many tests."

"Maybe it recharges naturally?" Elisa suggested another theory. "It's been a while since the final sacrifice."

"Not really. The crystals can hold spells and human Light for years."

"Are you sure it was one of your tests?"

"Well, it couldn't have happened naturally, as no woman wore it on her chest after the final ritual," he replied, narrowing his eyes. "You said that no one wore it, right?"

She nodded. "I wrapped it in a cloth and put it in my road bag. I made sure it was delivered to you safely."

He scratched his nose. "Well, unless this bag was on a horse's chest, and a horse is female –"

"No, nothing like that," Elisa reassured him, waving her hand. "It was on a dragon's chest."

They fell silent, staring at each other. Elisa's thoughts drifted back to Rose. The dragon had appeared normal for months until Kyle took her on a business trip. Julia was still in therapy, so he brought both dragons along to avoid leaving Rose alone. During the trip, Rose flew away for a week, and Kyle couldn't establish a mental connection with her. Eventually, she returned. Several weeks ago, Julia informed them that the mystery was solved when Rose laid three eggs.

"The dragon's eggs!" Edward exclaimed, grinning like a mad genius as he ran his hand through his messy hair. "The portal has just opened for them."

Elisa gave him a worried look. "What does it mean?"

"It means that we're on the threshold of something tremendous!" He gestured with his hands, trying to explain. "We conducted experiments on how it works with humans, but never with dragons. It appears that the portal opens just before the dragon's hutch. It could be influenced by the human spirit."

Elisa's eyes widened. "How exactly?!"

"I'm not sure. The dragon may possess the Gift of a deceased mage, for example. Or it could be nothing," Edward mused as he paced the room. "Regardless, I will go to the farm and observe them when they hatch."

Elisa chuckled. "Knowing you, I'm sure it's always something."

"Well, if I'm correct, then we'll find out," Edward said, unable to contain his excitement. "Now I have the opportunity to make a groundbreaking discovery in spiritual biology and potentially win the Huntz prize."

"Ed, you are so talented! You can win as many prizes as you want with your inventions."

"The Huntz prize is the most prestigious award in magic science. They don't hand it out for a pair of binoculars or an improved teapot design."

"What about your amazing Calling crystals?"

He lowered his eyes. "Well, for that one, I received a fascinating letter from the King."

"Really?" Elisa blinked and sat on a corner of the chair. "What did he say?"

He sighed. "I received a job offer in the special services. I'm sorry, but I'll be leaving our team soon."

"Stop apologizing! Such an offer is a once-in-a-lifetime opportunity. Plus, you truly deserve it."

"Maybe... but I've never been so far from home, away from all my friends and family."

"The Golden Palace is just two blocks away," Elisa reminded him. "We can still meet for a cup of coffee. And you can call me anytime if you feel lonely or bored."

"I think I didn't explain it properly. This was the letter from Esplendor."

She widened her eyes. "No way!"

The Esplendor Kingdom was renowned for its rich cultural life, attracting a diverse array of interesting individuals. It was a beautiful and luxurious place where famous artists, poets, writers, and actors chose to reside and create, thanks to the pleasant and warm weather year-round. In contrast, the Lake Kingdom was known for its scientists and ancient traditions.

The two kingdoms on the continent were always in competition, sometimes fostering healthy development through mutual encouragement, and other times resorting to tactics to entice valuable specialists to their side. And now, it was Ed.

Edward gave her a warm smile. "When I first met you at the Academy, I knew we would make a great team. And now I have to go. The offer they presented is just too good."

Elisa stood up and hugged him. "It's okay. I'm going to miss you, too."

"The Calling crystals won't work with such a great distance," he added, patting her shoulder. "So I'll write letters."

"I'll be glad to read them."

He nodded and turned to the shelves. "Actually, I have one more thing for you before I leave." He reached the highest shelf and retrieved one of his peculiar creations – a metal circle the size of a plate resting on a wooden frame with three legs. With pride, he placed it on his desk.

"What's that?"

He wiped the metal plate with a soft cotton ball. "I was trying to find a way to make the Calling crystals work over longer distances. Instead, I stumbled upon something strange." He walked to his drawer and opened the top shelf, revealing a crystal resting inside. Initially dull, it began to shine with an inner silver light as Edward brought it to the desk.

Elisa gave him a puzzled look. "What does it mean?"

"I tried using the new crystal, and I occasionally used the one we employed while attempting to catch the Incapables. Remember that day?"

Elisa nodded. It was difficult to forget that night when she sent Maya away, hoping she would lead them to her brother, the leader of a small teenage gang that had been robbing local jewelry stores. "Are you saying that you found them?"

"Not exactly. But when I hold the crystal like this, close to this amplifier, the connection with the ring is much stronger."

"So you can cast a Searching spell to locate them, right?"

"I attempted it, but it didn't work. The connection grew stronger, but the Searching spell only functions if the target is within ten miles, which is approximately sixteen kilometers. I believe that after we nearly caught them that day, they went into hiding, far from Middle Lake."

Elisa took the crystal in her hands. "How much stronger is the connection now?"

"Approximately three times stronger."

"So we know they are in the unreachable area, 10 miles from the Guardian House. But we also know that they are within 30 miles," Elisa said, her eyes filled with enthusiasm. "Do you have a map?"

He nodded in understanding and retrieved the map from the shelf. Clearing the desk of equipment, he unrolled the map of the Lake Kingdom. "Okay, let's work this out. First, let's visualize a 10-mile radius." Taking a pencil, he drew a circle around the Guardian House. Then, measuring 30 miles, he drew a larger circle around the same point.

Elisa pointed at the area between the two circles on the map. "Here they are."

"Well, actually, that's where the ring is," Edward corrected her. "And as we know, it was in Maya's winter coat. Now it's spring, so she might have left it where they stopped for the winter."

"Anyways, it's our best guess. Even if they stayed in someone's house and then left, we might find witnesses and trace their movements from there," Elisa said, determined not to give up. The prospect of closing this case was too enticing. She took the pencil and began marking possible hiding places for the Incapable teenagers.

To her relief, most of the area was occupied by lakes and mountains. The capital, Middle Lake, was situated on the shore of a vast lake that extended for miles to the south. In the west, there were caves and rivers with no human settlements. Thus, she drew an arc from the distant lakeshore to the edge of the forest.

"Here," Elisa said, using the pencil to point at the map. "If we position ourselves in the middle of this arc, we might have a chance to pick up the signal, locate the ring, and ultimately find the Incapables themselves."

"You're a really good detective," he complimented with a smile. "I think we can start right after Urchin returns from his trip."

Elisa hesitated. Urchin, her partner in this investigation, had gone south to visit his grandparents and was expected back in three days. She also had Walter, but he was preoccupied with wedding preparations and other robbery investigations.

"Should I really wait?" she asked. "It's not a vast area; it should only take a day or two at most."

"What if you do find them?" he pointed out. "You can't go alone. At the very least, take someone from the rookie team."

She shook her head. Despite being young and inexperienced herself just four years ago, she disliked working with inexperienced guardians. They were often too impulsive and could easily mess things up in an instant.

"You can ask Jackie," Edward suggested. "Now that we have Calling crystals, you can reach out to me anytime if you need help."

Elisa nodded. The journey wouldn't be too difficult, as there were several roads used by merchants to transport goods from surrounding farms. Additionally, it was the end of April, and the snow had melted. They might even enjoy this small forest trip with Jackie, if she agreed to it. Elisa would prefer her company over that of a newly graduated cadet. "Okay, I think it's settled then."

28

The Debut

Jackie scrolled through the pages of a freshly printed book. Its pages were pleasantly crispy and smelled of wood. There were pictures of different breeds of dragons with descriptions of their habitats, physical appearance, muscle power, and even character traits. When she reached the last page, she closed the book. The title read *How to Tame a Dragon*. It was hard to believe that it was only a project, an idea that they had started developing with Kyle just several months ago. And now, she held this very book in her hands.

"So what do you think?" Kyle asked. He sat in a chair in front of her desk. Today, he had just received his book copies and visited Jackie's office to share them.

Jackie smiled. "I love it. Especially the introduction."

"I took the letter that I wrote to Julia as a foundation. After all, this is why people should get a dragon in the first place – to protect the people they love." He lowered his eyes. "I've lost so many people already."

She nodded in understanding. Since his mother, Claudia, had passed away, falling into her own trap, it had been a difficult time for Kyle. He said that writing had helped him get through it and had become a sort of therapy.

"This book is absolutely beautiful," Jackie said. "And I'm so glad that you published it!"

"Me too. Now, we have a good chance to save the farm. It's interesting how things worked out. Last month, I traveled to two other kingdoms to collect more information on dragons, and I started talking to local farmers. Many of them became interested in raising dragons. So now I can go there and train them. I'll give them several copies of the book so they can continue this movement and attract more clients."

Jackie placed her book on the desk. "Aren't you afraid of competitors? It's a good and expensive business. If people around take it seriously, they might start selling dragons in packs. Then you might need to lower the prices."

He leaned back in his chair, his face calm. "Whatever. As long as it works and people are protected. I think the main victory is that I have an audience with the King this afternoon."

"He must say yes," Jackie encouraged him. "You've done a lot of work."

"Well, we all have," he said, clapping his briefcase, which was full of the petitions he had gathered.

Jackie smiled. After the case with the cult that they had resolved with Elisa, even the chief of the Middle Lake Guardian House agreed that a dragon, if trained wisely, could save many lives. Of course, Elisa had found a way to persuade him. She had also persuaded a guardian chief in Triville. In turn, Jackie had asked for signatures from all the people she knew, including Margaret and her *Daughters of Divine* community, where she was now a leader. With Theo, who had personally resolved multiple cases around the kingdom, and a journalist named Laura, who seemed to know everyone important in the city, they had gathered a solid amount of petitions.

Kyle gave her an excited look. "If the King agrees that I can professionally train the dragons for the army, it will be huge. We won't just save this idea and my farm. We will be able to reshape the world. Just imagine – how fast the guardians will fly to catch the criminals. With such an advantage, living and traveling will be much safer. And think of how many lives will be saved!"

Her heart fluttered in her chest. It was an honor to be a part of such a wonderful change.

Kyle took a pen from her desk. "So, should I sign a copy for you?"

"Of course." She moved the book closer to him, and Kyle opened it at the beginning. His hand moved quickly, leaving his words on the beige paper.

The door opened, and Elisa walked inside. She smiled upon seeing her old friend, Kyle, and they hugged.

"So, Kyle, congratulations on your debut," Elisa said as she sat in a chair.

"Thank you."

Elisa twisted a lock of her hair. "You know what, Ed is going to Esplendor, so I might give him a couple of book copies to give to their King."

"How does he know their King?" Jackie asked, caught by surprise.

Elisa shrugged. "He got a job offer from him, I guess, in a special lab. But it's a big secret, so he didn't give me the details."

"Well, Edward always was talented," Jackie agreed. "Impulsive at times, but with a genius, creative mind."

Kyle took three copies of his book from his box and gave them to Elisa. "Thank you for helping to spread the word."

Elisa opened the book from the top of the pile and scrolled through the pages randomly. "My pleasure. Trust me, this thing will spread as fast as a plague."

Jackie laughed. "What an awful comparison."

"I just hope it will go smoothly," Kyle said. "Please, keep your fingers crossed."

Elisa gave him a sly look. "You can always use the leverage."

"Which leverage?"

She gently touched the books that rested on her lap. "Say that we have serious connections in Esplendor, so they'll get scared that the West will take it to compete and gain more power."

He nodded. "I might use it as a last resort."

Jackie shook her head. "Unbelievable. We're talking about saving lives, and you're talking about this silly struggle for dominance."

Elisa shrugged. "It's politics. Since when do they care about anything other than dominance?"

Jackie couldn't find any words to object. Elisa never believed in human honesty and kindness, and sadly, she was often right. Like on the day they had saved Anna from sacrifice. Maybe it was silly of Jackie to believe in humanity, but she couldn't do it any other way.

"So when is the big hearing?" Elisa asked.

Kyle glanced at the time crystal on his wrist. It now glowed with a bright pink color. "In an hour. I probably should go."

She clapped his shoulder. "You will win. You always know what to say. It should go just fine."

"I hope so. I'll call you right away." He stood up and picked up his box of books before leaving.

When the door closed after him, Elisa gave Jackie an excited look. "How about we have a little forest journey this weekend?"

"Another journey?"

"Yes. Right after we celebrate Kyle's victory." Elisa took her hand, and it melted her anxiety away. Somehow, she knew that everything was going to be okay as long as Elisa was near.

"I would love that."

29

Flames of Passion

The branches crackled in the burning fire. Elisa extended her hands towards the flames to warm her palms. They had been on the road all day and found nothing so far. *Tomorrow will be another day. And I still can make the best of this one.*

Jackie brought a blanket, and they sat on it, wrapping the corners around themselves and hugging. The forest around them shone a pale green.

"I love these short romantic trips," Jackie said.

"Me too. Maybe it wasn't a bad idea to come here without guardians."

"What do you mean?" Jackie gave her an offended look. "I have some experience with undercover work. If I chose to be a guardian, I could be your partner."

Elisa kissed her forehead. "Dear, your change of career saved us from the need to hide. They wouldn't let us work together if you were a guardian."

"Unless we were married," Jackie reminded her.

Elisa didn't argue. Their marriage was another secret they kept from others. Only a few friends knew about the oaths they had exchanged on the bridge of wishes. It wasn't official paperwork, so Elisa always knew that no one would take it seriously. But Jackie was excited about it, and that was all that mattered.

"You know, since everything went well with Kyle and Julia, we should add to our small family," Jackie suggested.

"What do you mean? Did the story of the baby souls inspire you to consider adoption?"

"Honestly, no one will let us have a child," Jackie said, her voice tinged with sadness. "But that's not what I meant. I was actually thinking about getting our own dragon."

Elisa smiled. Since her flights with Rose, she had missed the feeling of soaring in the skies, far above the land and all of humanity with their never-ending problems.

She had thought about getting a dragon many times but never dared to speak about it, as nothing had been decided about Kyle and the farm. But now, it seemed possible. "I would love to do it. But dear, we live in a small rented apartment. Where would we keep it without risking burning down the whole neighborhood?"

"We could get a house in the suburbs, far away from all the neighbors," Jackie suggested.

Elisa nodded. Despite not earning much, they had some savings. Perhaps it was a good idea to get a house with their own yard where the baby dragon could play.

"Just imagine," Jackie continued to fuel her dreams. "The dragon could bring you many benefits at work – you might lead many investigations like this one. And we would have our own place with a garden and a big kitchen where I could cook for our friends and us. It would be so cool!"

"It would." Elisa hugged her tightly and gave her a long, passionate kiss.

The spring nights were still chilly, but Elisa felt almost sweaty when she was near Jackie. A flame of desire sparked somewhere in the depths of her belly, and she allowed it to grow. Her hands touched Jackie's neck and slid under her sweater, freeing her from the confines of heavy clothing. In Elisa's eyes, Jackie looked her best like this – in her natural, naked beauty.

Following her lead, Jackie undressed Elisa and pressed her bare skin against hers. Their hearts raced in unison as their sweaty bodies moved together in a passionate rhythm. Waves of pleasure rolled down their bodies, shaking them both.

As the sunrise approached, they lay under the covers, watching the stars fade. The trees gently shivered in the light wind, reflecting the flickers of the burning fire.

"You know what I realized today?" Jackie asked.

"What?" Elisa turned to her and rested her hand on her elbow.

"Kyle's story isn't just written in a book. What matters are all the deeds behind this manuscript. It's everything we did together to make a difference, to make someone's life better. It all started that day when we stole that dragon's eggs."

Elisa gently brushed a strand of hair from Jackie's forehead. "Back then, we were so naive. I only did it for Julia, to keep her safe."

"Maybe being naive isn't such a bad thing. If you think too far ahead, you lose sincerity. Just like Beth, the literary agent."

"True. And your manuscript isn't just a collection of memories. You make a much bigger impact with everything you do. You've helped so many people – Kyle, Julia, Margaret, Anna. Not to mention all those women who found help and shelter," Elisa said, locking eyes with Jackie. "We live in times of significant change. These days, actions speak louder than words."

Jackie's eyes sparkled as she touched the heart-shaped pendant she always carried on her neck. "I love you so much."

"And I love you," Elisa replied, kissing her. "Let's get some sleep now."

Jackie closed her eyes and turned to her other side, allowing Elisa to hug her from behind. Before drifting off, Elisa glanced at the crystal Edward had given her to check the connection with the ring. It had always rested on her horse's neck. To her surprise, it was now alive, glowing with a bright silver light.

Elisa sat up and blinked several times to ensure it wasn't a dream. The connection with the ring was strong, indicating that someone carrying it was approaching their location.

She shook Jackie's shoulder to wake her up. "What's happening?" Jackie moaned, not opening her eyes.

"The ring," Elisa said, jumping to her feet. "We've found it."

Jackie turned onto her back and rubbed her heavy eyelids. "Why now?" she asked, addressing her fate.

"If Walter's ring is nearby, so are the Incapables."

Her words prompted Jackie to sit up. "Should we go there?"

"They are very close but on the move. We might lose this trail if we don't go right away."

Jackie didn't need more explanation. Without wasting any words, she put on her boots and extinguished the fire. During this time, Elisa prepared the Searching spell, and the crystal illuminated with a blue light. It hovered, ready to lead them to their target.

30

The Ring

The sunrise illuminated the corner of the sky as the trail led them to the foggy river shore. In the distance, they could hear the voices of a group of people. Elisa and Jackie dismounted their horses and concealed them behind the trees to avoid drawing attention.

They made their way through the trees, their trunks adorned with fading mint-green bark. When they reached a wide oak, they stopped. Elisa squinted, noticing a thin pinkish-gray fog that revealed the silhouettes of two women washing clothes in the streaming water. On the shore, another woman was folding the freshly washed garments into wicker baskets.

Elisa furrowed her brow, sensing that something was amiss. There were a couple of unanswered questions: *Why were these women at the shore at such an early hour? And why was there no blue coat among the pile of clothes?* "Maya isn't here," she remarked. "And her coat is missing."

"So what?" Jackie shrugged. "Someone might come across this expensive ring and decide to keep it."

Elisa let out a heavy sigh. "It's heartbreaking how they take everything valuable from these children."

Jackie gave her a curious look. "You seem to have a strong connection to her."

"We share a similar background," Elisa explained. It was true – both Maya and herself were orphans. Who could steal from an orphan? Only someone heartless. And it was one of these women.

"Actually, it's not her ring," Jackie reminded her. "It belongs to Walter."

"Regardless, let's retrieve it."

Stepping onto the shore, Elisa raised her palm, a ball of electricity crackling in her hand. It grew brighter, catching the attention of the women who turned to face them. Elisa and Jackie stood before them.

"Where is the ring?" Elisa demanded.

The women exchanged glances but remained silent.

Elisa shifted the electric ball from one hand to the other. "Don't underestimate me, ladies. I'm a guardian, and I know that one of you has taken the diamond ring from Maya. It was hidden in her blue winter coat."

One of the women let out a sigh and retrieved the ring from her pocket. Her pale fingers trembled as she held it, the diamond catching the light from Elisa's electric ball.

Jackie approached the woman, taking the ring from her grasp. She then returned to Elisa's side and whispered in her ear, "I don't like them. Let's leave now."

Elisa shook her head, lowering her voice. "They may have information about Maya and the rest of the group. You can use your Gift to investigate. Can you do that?"

Jackie's eyes widened. "I can, but –"

"At least, we can determine if Maya and Eric are still around."

Jackie looked at Elisa with fear in her eyes. "What if these women start screaming and alert the others?"

"They are just Incapables," Elisa reassured her. "And they fear us. Besides, they have already seen us, so we have nothing to lose."

Jackie sighed. "I hope you're right."

Elisa nodded confidently and took a step forward. "You three, tell us quickly where Maya is, the girl you stole from. And where is her brother?"

The woman who had handed over the ring furrowed her brow. "They are in a nearby village. Have they broken any rules?"

"Yes," Jackie interjected, standing by Elisa's side with her arms crossed.

"Now, you will allow us to quickly check you. Is that clear?" Elisa demanded.

The woman nodded in agreement.

"Good," Elisa said.

The next thing she knew, a sharp pain shot through her neck, and darkness enveloped her.

As Elisa regained consciousness, she found herself seated in a barn, bound to a wooden pillar with ropes that dug into her wrists. The throbbing pain in her neck served as a stark reminder of the needle that had likely been coated with a sleeping potion. "Damn Incapables," she muttered.

Jackie was also tied to a nearby pillar, fast asleep with her chest rising and falling rhythmically. Elisa breathed a sigh of relief. They were both alive, giving them a glimmer of hope for escape.

The barn door creaked open, and a tall young man in a gray shirt entered. His bright blue eyes mirrored Maya's, leaving no doubt that he was her brother, Eric. A light stubble dusted his cheeks, a telltale sign of his youth. *Damn, he's younger than me!*

Eric glanced at the sleeping Jackie before turning his attention to Elisa. "How foolish of you to come here alone."

"We aren't alone," Elisa lied. "If we do not return by sunrise, the guardians will descend upon this place and reduce it to ashes."

Eric chuckled, twirling a diamond ring between his fingers. "We spotted you in the forest last night. I'm well aware that no one will come to your rescue. In truth, we anticipated your arrival and set this little trap."

Elisa's heart sank. Apart from the unsettling thought that their intimate encounter may have been witnessed, the revelation of an Incapables spy was concerning. It was evident that their gang possessed a well-organized structure, capable of luring them to the village using the ring. Eric posed a significant threat.

"How did you discover that we were searching for you?" Elisa asked.

"In the winter, when you stormed into our laboratory, I began to suspect something was amiss. I realized you had found a way to track us, especially after witnessing how you allowed my sister to escape that night," Eric explained.

Elisa blinked in surprise. Despite societal prejudices, this Incapable displayed intelligence. If he possessed magical abilities, he could have been a skilled detective or a formidable villain. The age-old adage echoed in her mind like a belated, sardonic warning: *Never underestimate your enemy.*

"I found this in her coat." Eric tossed the ring at her feet, the sound of it clinking against the stone floor. "I could have disposed of it, but I opted to use it as bait to lure you here."

"What do you mean?"

Leaning in closer, Eric brushed his rough fingers against her chin. His breath, tinged with the aroma of dark coffee, wafted over her face. "You are merely a foolish woman, Elisa. You seem to enjoy talking, so you will divulge everything you know."

Elisa scowled at his sexist comment. In this regard, he was no different from most male mages. "How do you know my name?"

Eric chuckled. "If you valued secrecy, you should not have confided in Maya."

Elisa gritted her teeth. Maya... Was she merely a frightened child who divulged everything to her brother, or was she an enemy? Elisa chided herself for feeling sympathy towards her.

Kneeling before Elisa, Eric placed his hands on her lap. "Now, tell me what you know about us."

Instead of responding, Elisa spat in his face.

Eric calmly wiped away the saliva and rose to his feet. Retrieving a sharp knife from his belt, he approached Jackie. Elisa's breath caught in her throat.

His eyes glinted with malice. "I wanted to hurt *you*, but now we'll resort to more drastic measures. Speak, or I'll kill your lover."

"Please, no," Elisa's voice quivered. "We're aware that you have stolen copper, and that night we discovered you were constructing some devices. However, we never determined their exact nature."

"Are you certain?" Eric pressed, holding the knife against Jackie's delicate skin. The silver chain around her neck glinted in the sunlight. Jackie wore a magical heart necklace symbolizing their enduring love, and with the blade so close to her neck, Elisa was willing to divulge anything to ensure her safety.

"Fine, we uncovered something. Our specialist examined a device that survived the fire. We believe they are designed to capture and transmit voices over a distance."

"Fuck," Eric cursed, rising and venting his frustration by kicking the haystack.

Elisa remained composed, recalling Jackie's advice that people often made rash decisions when consumed by anger. Fortunately, such emotions tended to be short-lived.

Turning back to Elisa, Eric demanded, "What else do you know?"

"That's all," Elisa replied, her eyes welling up. "Truly, that's the extent of our knowledge. We sought you out to understand the purpose behind these devices."

Furrowing his brow, Eric questioned, "What are your thoughts on their purpose?"

Elisa's breaths came in heavy, labored gasps. A sudden realization dawned upon her. The crystals that Edward had invented, operating on the same principle, had significantly enhanced communication among the guardians of the entire Lake Kingdom within a few months. It had revolutionized their efficiency and effectiveness. But *what if the Incapables possess a similar means of communication?* It could explain how their spy maintained contact with the rest of the gang over vast distances.

Further implications began to form in Elisa's mind, each more troubling than the last. *What if they aren't just isolated gangs but multiple well-organized factions of activists? What if they are collaborating on a clandestine plan, orchestrating a silent rebellion movement?* Elisa bit her lip. Voicing any of these suspicions aloud could lead to Eric killing them both. Silent and contemplative, Elisa kept her thoughts to herself.

"Don't dwell on it too much," Eric warned, twirling the knife in his hand. "You will remain here until tomorrow. I'll determine your fate then."

With that, he departed, leaving Elisa and Jackie alone in the dimly lit barn. The door closed behind him, enveloping them in darkness, with only faint sunbeams filtering through the worn roof.

Gradually, Elisa's eyes adjusted to the subdued light. She turned to Jackie, noticing a slight cut on her neck where Eric's knife had grazed her. The bleeding had ceased, and Jackie was no longer in immediate danger. For now, that was enough of a relief.

31

A Promise

Jackie's eyelids fluttered, and she opened her eyes. The room she was in was dark, and she couldn't move. She was sitting on the ground, her body stiff. She blinked several times before her vision focused on the dark silhouette near her. "Lissy?" she called in a whisper.

"My dear, don't be afraid," Elisa said in a quiet, gentle voice. "You slept all day, but now we'll figure out how to get out of here."

Jackie moved her tied hands and tried to release them, but it didn't help. "Are they gonna kill us?"

Elisa paused before replying. "Not right now. We have time to find the way out."

"Damn it. If only I had listened to my gut and left right after we got the ring back!"

"It's not your fault," Elisa's voice was soft and reassuring. "This guy, Eric, just came here. He said they discovered the ring long ago, and their spies were on the road all this time. They were expecting the guardians to start looking for them again. It was a trap. If we hadn't found those women, they would have attacked us anyway. In the morning, probably."

Tears filled her eyes. She leaned over the pillar and looked at the ceiling. Among the cracks, there was a darkening sky. "We will die here. They won't let us go."

"Don't say that," Elisa's voice sounded from the dark. "We both were in much worse situations, and we got out of all of them. Never give up!"

Jackie blinked to chase the tears away. *What if this is it?* It was the law of life – even the most incredible luck had its limits, and in the depth of her soul, she always knew it. A sadness pressed on her chest like a giant stone.

She needed to speak it out. To say everything to Elisa until death did them part. "You know, I could have died several years ago, but I was saved and got into the Academy where I met you. Then we got involved in that Moondust case, and I got another chance to live again. I'm grateful that I used it wisely and chose to stay with you. All these years, you were the most valuable part of my life. I always loved you with all my heart, and I always will." Her voice trembled, and the tears rolled down her cheeks. Jackie couldn't even wipe them, but she didn't care about her looks. She took a deep breath and continued. "I only regret the time that we wasted, hesitating. When we pretended to be someone else."

"Jackie, it's not the end. Not now," Elisa made a quiet sob, opposing her own words. "We have so many things to do in life! You must publish your book, and we'll get our own place. And a cute dragon. We will soar in the skies on it, not caring about the rest of the world."

Jackie closed her eyes. Once, when they stole the dragons, she dreamed of becoming one. At that time, she was totally broken, not seeing anything in this world but endless human cruelty. She wanted to escape, to become free. She managed to deal with it because of her friends and because of unconditional love that healed all her wounds. It let her learn that true freedom meant the ability to be herself.

"Please, don't give up on our dreams," Elisa asked. Her voice was too weak.

"I won't," Jackie promised only to calm her.

For a minute, they were sitting in front of each other in the darkness, tied to the opposite pillars. The ropes, soaked with some greasy potion, were blocking their magic channels. Despite that, Jackie felt so good just sitting by Elisa's side. It was bliss that she happened to have this person in her life.

The barn door opened, filling it with candlelight. It was Maya. She held a lantern in her hand, and it lit up her concentrated face as she stepped inside.

Elisa breathed out. "I'm so glad that you're alright –"

"Don't you dare to say that after you lied to me!" Maya glanced at Jackie and frowned. "I know you. You pretended to be a seller when you gave me that coat in a store. How could you do that?"

Jackie lowered her eyes without having an answer. Maya was right – they betrayed her trust, so the chance she would help them escape was too small.

Elisa's voice softened. "Maya, I'm so sorry. The guardians just wanted to speak to your brother, but we would never hurt you."

Maya scoffed. "Really?!"

"I swear with my own life."

Maya stood where she was. *She doesn't walk away, which is a good sign*, Jackie observed. Despite her blocked magic channels, Jackie was still a mind reader and a master of words. Intuitively, she knew what to do in harsh situations like this, so she let herself rely on her experience. Jackie looked at her as an expert, trying to guess what was on her mind. Firstly, Maya was cautious, which might mean she came here out of curiosity, probably without anyone's permission. Secondly, she was a child, and she might still be a believer. It might be a good card to play.

Jackie gave her an intriguing look. "I know what your biggest dream is."

"No, you don't," Maya said, frowning. "You must touch people to read them."

Jackie didn't blink. Maya's knowledge of her mind-reading Gift didn't change anything. She also knew some of her story, especially about her biggest trauma. "You want to get your parents back."

Maya went silent, her lips partly opened. The mixture of curiosity and doubt stood in her wide-opened blue eyes. *Then I guessed correctly.*

Jackie locked her eyes with hers. "Unfortunately, no magic can avert death, but you know what? Love heals all wounds, even this deep. It fills your soul with light and gives you a new understanding of life itself."

Maya came closer, the lantern bouncing in her small hands and casting long, crooked shadows along the walls. "Who will ever love me?"

"At first, never say that. Everyone deserves to be loved. I can help you find your destiny. The necklace I currently wear has a special power – it can lead you to your true love. And you can take it."

Maya glanced at Elisa, then back at Jackie. "But what about you?"

She gave her a warm smile. "I've already found my true love, and she is right here. So I'm giving this necklace to you, Maya. As a gift."

Maya gave them both a perplexed look. "Do you really love each other?"

"Yes," Elisa confirmed. "More than anything."

"I guess the price for this gift is your freedom?" Maya asked.

Jackie shrugged. "Only sincere and honest people can find and keep their true love. If you set us free, you will do a good deed. According to the Divine law, you will be rewarded."

Maya took a small knife out of her pocket. "Are you sure?"

Jackie flinched. *Was I too pushy?* This Incapable girl could easily stab the knife in her throat. She took a deep breath, praying that her luck would not let her down till the end. "I believe that you'll make the right choice."

Maya leaned over Jackie and cut the power ropes on her hands.

After the ropes fell off, Jackie rubbed her wrists. Then she removed her necklace and let Maya take it.

The girl put it into her inner pocket. Then she turned to Elisa and started removing her ropes.

"Why are you really helping us?" Elisa asked her.

"I just don't want you to die like this. Even though you lied to me, you deserve a second chance." Maya sighed. "Eric said he must kill you in the morning."

She said it with such a flat tone that Jackie's heart sank.

"What if he noticed that you helped us?" Jackie asked.

She shrugged. "I'll play stupid. As usual."

They walked to the northern gates, where Maya had pointed. The sun had already set, and darkness covered them like a shield. The villagers were mostly at home, the windows in their huts illuminated by candlelight. Elisa and Jackie hid behind the corner of a house when one of the Incapable men passed by. As Maya had warned them, he was on duty that night.

When the street became clear, they ran to the gates and walked outside. The forest stood before them, shimmering mint green in silence. Elisa stopped, thinking. Her intuition let her down sometimes, but when she had this soaking feeling of real danger, it was always something to think of. It was easy to believe that Maya helped them escape, but at the same time, it would be too naive. Girls like her were never so naive. Elisa knew it because she was just the same. *Then why would they let us go?*

She held her breath, thinking. They didn't want to kill them in a village, that's why. Death left an energy mark that never melted unless someone erased it. Incapables didn't have the power to erase the spells. And if the guardians discovered such marks in a village, the Incapables would be in serious trouble. It would be more convenient if the guardians found their dead bodies far from the village, somewhere in the forest. Incapables didn't leave energy traces, so they would never find the killers.

Jackie pulled her elbow. "Let's go."

"No. It's another trap."

Jackie raised her hand, and her blue Light sparkled in her palm. "So what? We have our magic now."

Elisa nodded, and they slowly walked to the forest trail. They managed to make twenty steps when five Incapables surrounded them. Eric was in the middle as their leader. Two men held the pipes – it was the same weapon they had used on them before. Elisa bet these pipes contained the same poisoned needles, but this time she was fully ready to protect herself and Jackie.

Eric stepped forward, grinning. "Are you going somewhere?"

Elisa and Jackie exchanged looks in silence. Good that they were trained to handle situations like this. It took a split second for them to take a defensive position. Jackie stepped behind her back, and Elisa raised her hands. The waves of electricity burst from her fingers, and they melted the needles that flew towards them. The pieces of steel fell on the ground before even reaching them.

Then Elisa moved her hands across, and the lightning beams reached the men, wrapping them like a shining spider net. She took a deep breath to concentrate. All five of them shook, hit by her magic. She held them for several seconds until her head started spinning.

Elisa dropped her hands down, and the men fell to the ground. She fell on her knees, breathless.

Jackie ran to Eric and checked the pulse on his neck. "Alive. You managed to knock them out."

Elisa took several short breaths before she could reply. Knocking out five adult men, even Incapables, appeared to be very exhausting. "Tie him. We must bring him to Middle Lake for interrogation."

To be able to carry him, Jackie took Eric by the shoulders, and Elisa took his feet. He was a heavy man, and they stopped several times before they reached the river shore. Their horses were still at rest there, chewing the fresh grass.

This exercise drained all the energy from Elisa. When they finally tied Eric and put him on Jackie's horse, the moon rose in the sky, and she was about to faint.

Jackie touched her shoulder, a worry crossing her face. "You are so pale."

"It's just moonlight." Elisa waved her hand dismissively. "Let's go."

"We must be cautious. It's dangerous to ride a horse in the dark."

Elisa mounted her horse, fighting with her shaking feet. "Don't worry. It's spring, so the trail is well-lit, and the path is smooth."

She smiled. "Can you imagine Urchin's face when he sees us? He must be back tomorrow."

"Yeah." Elisa mustered a smile. Urchin had no idea about their small adventure, and he probably would be mad at her because she put Jackie in such danger. Elisa would be glad to call someone from their team to warn them or ask to meet them halfway to be sure that Incapables wouldn't chase them. Alas, these people took her Calling crystal away.

She couldn't even send a Light signal because they were too far away from Middle Lake. Also, they didn't have time to waste. Her Gift release took too much energy, and she still had to ride. At least, for a couple of hours until they could be sure that the Incapables weren't chasing them.

Elisa took the reins and clasped her horse's sides. Jackie rode after her with Eric.

32

Last Wish

They rode until the horizon became a bright gray. The new day was windy, bringing heavy clouds that covered the sky. Jackie followed Elisa's quiet pace, as it was too dangerous to move fast. The nocturnal nature was slowly falling asleep, and its gentle beauty was dimming. The moss on the trees stopped shining, and the wildflowers closed their buds.

Jackie tried to enjoy the ride despite all her concerns, but now, when the morning light revealed Elisa's silhouette, it was hard to ignore the obvious. Apparently, she was exhausted – Elisa bounced too much in her saddle as her hands barely held the reins. Stubborn Elisa refused to make a brief stop for a nap.

Eventually, her head tilted too much, and she slid from her saddle, falling onto the ground. Jackie stopped in the middle of the road and rushed to help her sit up.

"What's happened?" Elisa asked, her dark-blue eyes blurred.

Jackie wiped a smear of mud from her cheek. "You fell asleep. Good thing you didn't break anything!"

Elisa touched her forehead. "Shit. I'm so sorry. I'll try to focus this time." She rose to her feet, but Jackie stepped between Elisa and the horse. "No more riding! You are too worn out!"

"But Incapables –"

"No more Incapables!" Jackie crossed her arms. "We are in a safe zone, just a couple of hours from the city. Plus, I saw the glade nearby. Please lay on the damn blanket for an hour, and then we'll continue the ride."

Elisa glanced at dozing Eric, who was safely tied to the back of Jackie's saddle. "Fine. But give this guy some sleeping potion. I have some leftovers in my roadbag."

"Okay."

In the glade, Jackie gave Elisa a rolled blanket and sent her to make herself a bed at the firepit. She reached into Elisa's bag to find a potion. Surprised, she found a book, *How to Tame a Dragon*. She turned to Elisa. "Why do you carry that with you?"

Elisa yawned. "I was going to give it to Edward, remember? And I forgot about it as we left the next morning."

Jackie shook her head. "You should keep it safe."

She chuckled. "Right. Like Incapables would use it to start raising dragons."

"Why not?"

"They don't have magic for that." Elisa lay down and covered herself with the other half of her blanket. "Mental power, of course. I could use my mental power to call Rose. She would hear me from anywhere."

Jackie placed the book back and sat near Elisa. "Please, save this energy for our short ride home. Sleep well now."

"Jackie, give him more potion. He mustn't wake up." Elisa's heavy eyelids started to close.

"Don't worry. I'm on duty now." Jackie placed a gentle kiss on her soft lips.

"I love you," she whispered.

"I love you too."

When Elisa fell into a slumber, Jackie shrugged from the cold gust of wind. The day promised to be nasty, and it would be good to make a small fire for her to prevent catching a cold. She stood up and walked to find the Sleeping potion for Eric.

The bottle was at the very bottom, hidden in a small leather bag. When Jackie finally managed to take it, she discovered it was empty. Somehow, the lid fell off and soaked the bag from inside. The smell made her dizzy. Jackie pulled it away from her face. The worst thing would be to fall asleep in the middle of her duty. She glanced at Eric. He was still asleep and tied well, which meant he wasn't dangerous. She shrugged and went into the forest to find some wood brush.

In ten minutes, Jackie was back in the glade. She placed her wood brush into the firepit and checked on Elisa – she was sleeping quietly. Jackie smiled and shifted her eyes to the horses. Eric wasn't there. Only the ropes were on the ground, like a silent reminder of her carelessness. Her heart skipped a beat.

The cold metal touched her neck. Eric was behind her, his hot breath reaching her ears. "One move, and this needle will pierce your artery."

Jackie breathed heavily. Her throat became dry at once, and she could hardly stand on her feet. "Please, just take a horse and go."

He chuckled. "And what next? Like you'll stop chasing me."

Damn, he is like a cat who caught a silly mouse. He enjoyed playing with her nerves. Jackie summoned all her stamina to focus on her shaking hands. She was still a mage. If she placed her palms to-gether, she could cast a Paralyzing spell.

Preventing her next move, his free hand grasped her wrist tightly and pulled her hand behind her back. "Don't even think of it."

She swallowed hard. "What do you want?"

"I've heard you have a book about dragons. I think I can make use of it."

"Since when are you awake?"

He sneered. "It's none of your concern. So where is the book?"

"In Elisa's road bag," Jackie said in a grave voice.

"Then I'll take it. And her horse."

"Fine," she agreed. "Will you go now?"

He laughed into her ear, deafening her. "Okay, as you were so cooperative, I'll let you choose who will stay alive today. You or her?"

Jackie's eyes filled with tears. When she and Elisa spoke about such scenarios as cadets, Jackie confessed that she would never choose herself to save. Nothing had changed since, but one thought occurred to her just now – *Will Elisa ever be okay without me?* Elisa always said that she couldn't imagine her life without Jackie, and she asked to spare her life if Jackie had to.

Leaving Elisa like this was unbearable. But at least she would be alive. Deep inside, Jackie always knew that Elisa was strong. Much stronger than anyone Jackie knew. Maybe her heart would break, but one day Elisa could live again.

"Think faster," he pressed his metal pipe to her neck. "Time is fading."

"Kill me."

"Really?" His voice was full of disbelief. "Think again. You can live a good, long life."

"I need your guarantee that you won't touch her," Jackie said, her voice surprisingly plain.

"You have my word." He took a step back. "On your knees."

She kneeled to the ground and closed her eyes, ready to drift away. Something tickled her neck. *A needle?* Her thoughts mixed up, and she fell to the ground, lying on her side. The gust of the wind brought the smells of the flowers. *The world is so cruel,* was her last thought, *but nature is so beautiful.*

A cold rain droplet fell on her forehead, and Elisa opened her eyes. She blinked, trying to chase the unpleasant sensation away. Then another raindrop fell on her nose. She sat up. The leftovers of the ropes that they used to tie Eric were in the fire pit. Jackie lay on the ground nearby, her face peaceful. *Is she asleep?*

Elisa turned to check the horses – Jackie's horse was tied to the tree. Hers was gone together with Eric. The hoofs clattered far away, between the trees. Elisa jumped to her feet and ran forward, moving her hand and making a shot. The lightning hit the trees, unable to reach him.

"Fuck!" She shouted.

The rain straightened in response, watering the path between them. Elisa's heart was racing. She could come back and take another horse to try to chase him, but it would be too risky if his friends were moving in their direction. It would be better to come back to this village later with Urchin and the other guys. Plus, she needed to wake Jackie up.

Elisa turned to the glade. Jackie was motionless.

"I've told you to give him a potion," Elisa grumbled, moving closer. "He is Incapable, but he is too strong." Elisa sat near Jackie, and only then did she notice how pale her face was. The heavy rain droplets, the size of diamonds, kept falling on her cold skin. Her heart sank. Jackie wasn't breathing.

She shook her shoulders with trembling hands, but Jackie didn't open her eyes. Her fingers touched a steel needle that pierced her neck. Elisa froze, unable to believe that the love of her life was dead. Elisa kept sitting like this, paralyzed by shock. Her blood heavily pumped in her veins. The thoughts twisted in her head like sparkles, and then they melted in the dark. The words from The Book of Gifts pierced her chest. "*The healer's Gift is rare. Limitations – death more than five minutes, romantic feelings … This Gift might heal only once.*"

She gently put Jackie back on the ground. Then Elisa closed her eyes and screamed as loud as she could.

She kept wailing until her voice became hoarse. Then she fell back on the cold, wet grass. The sharp pain squeezed her laughs, and the rain poured, nailing her to the ground. She wished she would die, but she kept breathing.

Elisa had no idea how long she had been lying like this. When the rain stopped, a crow circled in the sky over her, and Elisa closed her eyes not to see the skies. Not to know anything. Not to live in this world where life was so fucking unfair.

33

Her Eyes

The bridge of wishes hung over the streaming river, with time crystals mounted into the metal railings glowing a dark-blue color. It reminded Elisa of Jackie's Light, consuming her thoughts. The color of the crystals indicated it was seven in the evening, but time held no significance for her. Time had stopped for her on the day she lost Jackie.

Walking to the middle of the bridge, Elisa leaned over the railings. The tired sun hung low over the horizon, casting a warm light on the treetops ahead. Soon, this light would fade, enveloping the town in darkness.

Elisa reached into her pocket and touched a metal object. She took out the diamond ring and stared blankly at it. It was Walter's ring, the one she had picked up before leaving the barn in the village of Incapables with Jackie. She had completely forgotten about it until now.

She exhaled a heavy sigh, a wave of sadness washing over her. This ring was meant for a happy couple, but instead, it had brought nothing but pain and regret. Tears welled in her eyes as she sobbed, clutching the ring tightly in her hand. Then she hurled it as far as she could. It gleamed briefly before disappearing into the river below.

Elisa wished for the ring to be consumed by the depths of the river, along with all the happy couples who had the luxury of living their lives without the burden of loss and heartache.

Her hands clenched the railings as she looked up at the pale moon rising in the dark-blue skies. Memories of winter vacation with Jackie flooded her mind, of making wishes under cascading snowfall. *All I want is to be with you. Always. Whatever happens next.* This was what she had whispered to Jackie that day.

How naive she had been! More than anything, Elisa longed to bring Jackie back, to gaze into her magnificent green eyes once more. But it was an impossible wish. A shiver rolled down her spine. Unable to contain her grief, Elisa dropped her face into her palms, sobbing until her eyes ran dry.

As she gazed at the dark horizon, a new wish formed in her heart. "I want to find Eric and make him pay for everything he did."

A quiet rustle caught her attention, and she turned her head to the left. A small creature approached her by the railings, its appearance puzzling. Elisa wiped her eyes to get a clearer look. It was a small dragon, with cute wings and charcoal scales.

The dragon drew closer, its beautiful green eyes meeting Elisa's. Her heart sank as she realized they were Jackie's eyes.

"Hi there," Elisa greeted the dragon, gently petting its head as it purred under her touch. A smile graced her lips, perhaps for the first time in weeks.

Approaching footsteps caught her attention, and she turned to see Julia, her loyal friend, standing by her side. Julia had set everything aside to be there for Elisa during this difficult time.

For Elisa, the events following that cursed day when Jackie died were shrouded in a fog of confusion. She recalled the voices that surrounded her in the days that followed. First, Walter and Urchin had arrived at the glade where the tragedy occurred. The night before, the guardians had grown concerned when Elisa ceased responding to the Calling crystal, eventually finding her using a Searching spell.

Julia had been the one to assist Elisa in changing her clothes and eating, providing much-needed support during those dark days. On the day Elisa collected Jackie's ashes, they held a farewell ceremony attended by numerous guardians, teachers, and individuals who had been touched by Jackie's kindness and inspiration. Elisa felt a sense of unease as she held the urn, preparing to bury it in the ground according to their traditions. The act of saying goodbye felt surreal, leaving everything devoid of purpose.

It was Julia who suggested burying Jackie's ashes in Triville, the place where they had exchanged vows. As Elisa laid the ashes to rest in the earth, she felt a shift within herself, a newfound ability to venture out alone without needing coaxing from her bed.

Approaching Elisa, Julia gazed at her with warm hazel eyes. "Here you are."

Elisa gestured towards the dragon. "Are you talking to me or this cutie?"

Julia reached out to touch the dragon, scratching its cheek. "Who escaped again? Who's a naughty girl?"

The dragon emitted a soft moan, eliciting smiles from both Elisa and Julia.

"Why is she so small?" Elisa inquired, breaking the silence.

"This little one was born just three weeks ago when..." Julia's voice trailed off.

Elisa let out a sigh. "It's been three weeks already?"

"Time never stops," Julia remarked, placing her hand on Elisa's. "By the way, Walter called. He agreed that you can stay here as long as you need."

"I don't know if I can go back there, honestly. To our empty apartment," Elisa's voice trembled, trailing off.

"Let's not dwell on that now," Julia said calmly, redirecting her attention to the dragon, which had now stretched out on the railing as if it were the perfect place to rest. "Kyle improved the gate on the barn, but she's quite curious and keeps finding a way to escape. Somehow, she found her way to you, and I think she's taken a liking to you."

"Does she?!" Elisa's eyes widened in surprise.

Julia nodded solemnly. "Certainly. And for you to know, if the dragon takes a liking to you, it's significant. They choose their masters."

Elisa closed her tired eyes. "We used to dream of having a dragon. And a place with a big backyard."

"I think this is what you need right now," Julia suggested, patting her shoulder. "What if you stay here for the summer? You can help raise her."

Elisa gently stroked the dozing dragon and gazed at the silver curve of the river. "I might. Even though I don't believe it will help me overcome my loss."

Julia placed her hand on her chest. "Honestly, nothing truly helps. As a healer, I've learned that the worst physical wounds often hurt much less than the ones left in our souls. I've seen many patients who continued to suffer long after I healed them."

"Why?"

"Because sometimes they were the only ones who survived the fire, for example, while the rest of their family was gone. They couldn't forgive themselves for outliving them."

"Just like me," Elisa said, lowering her gaze. She found herself able to speak of it now. "I foolishly fell asleep. I was supposed to protect her –"

"You were exhausted and could have fallen from the horse and broken your neck," Julia reasoned.

"I wish I had." Elisa sighed. "I instructed Jackie to give him a Sleeping potion, but he must have awakened before that and shot her... All this time, I can't shake the thought – why did he spare me to suffer?"

"He's just a despicable person," Julia offered sympathetically. "While this tragedy may have ended Jackie's physical life, her spirit will endure forever. In our hearts, memories, and in all the good she ever did. The program I underwent, the female circle... It truly aided in my healing after my own loss." Tears welled up in Julia's eyes. "I've spoken with local women, and I aim to continue this program here in Triville and beyond. I will ensure it thrives because it's a force for good, and nothing will deter me. We will honor her memory and keep it alive."

Elisa embraced Julia. "Thank you. It means a great deal to me."

"You're always welcome to join us," Julia assured, wrapping her arms around Elisa's shoulders.

They stood in silence, and Elisa closed her eyes to absorb the weight of the moment. Perhaps she was a terrible friend to Julia.

She wasn't there for her in her times of need. But now, when they stood together, sharing their grief, the burden was a bit lighter to bear.

Julia leaned back, wiping her face before taking a deep breath. "Elisa, I understand that this dragon can never replace Jackie, but she was born on the day Jackie passed. Some souls enter this world to watch over us, to guide us forward."

Elisa pondered Julia's words. Maybe Edward had been right about the spiritual portal. Perhaps it wasn't Jackie herself, but after her passing, her spirit could have connected with the dragon's, serving as a protector for Elisa. It was even possible that the dragon had inherited Jackie's Gift.

Elisa opened her arms, allowing the dragon to leap onto her chest.

"I know nothing about these creatures," Elisa said.

"I'll teach you. That's what we do here."

Gently hugging the dragon, Elisa stroked its dark scales. "What shall we name you, little one?"

"I think we both know the answer," Julia said.

"Then welcome to the family, Jackie," Elisa declared with a smile.

The dragon purred and emitted a chomping sound, and in that moment, Elisa could breathe again.

Epilogue

The sun was kissing the horizon as Elisa left the barn. She shaded her eyes and gazed at the golden clouds floating in the quiet evening sky. Soon, she would soar there with her dragon. When Elisa shared this dream with her beloved Jackie, she never imagined it would come true in such a peculiar way.

Today, Jackie, her dragon, couldn't fall asleep quickly, fussing and demanding attention. At six months old and the size of a small horse, Jackie was on the cusp of puberty. Elisa sometimes worried that Jackie's behavior wasn't just mood swings; she might inherit a mind-reading Gift. If Jackie could read the minds of everyone who touched her, she could be shocked or even traumatized.

That's why Elisa decided to stay in Triville, where the crime rate was considerably lower. She considered quitting her guardian career but, after a long discussion with Theo, agreed only to reduce her hours. Sometimes, Elisa worked alongside Theo and other team members, and these new connections and experiences helped her heal, slowly but steadily.

The sound of horse hooves jolted her from her daydream. Elisa turned to face the horseman. He was riding to her, his gorgeous golden cloak fluttering in the air, reflecting the sunshine. He wore a black uniform, with the dragon perched on his right shoulder. Which meant he wasn't from around here. It was the guardian from Esplendor, a western Kingdom. *What is he doing here?*

Elisa placed her bucket on the ground and shook the hay from her polka-dot dress. With her hair untied and unbrushed, she probably looked like a neglected village woman.

The guardian approached and dismounted his black stallion. Elisa hardly recognized him. His light hair was brushed back and tied in a knot, making him appear ten years older. But his face was too familiar, as she had seen him almost every day before she left Middle Lake.

"Ed!" Elisa rushed to give him a tight hug.

"I missed you too, cowgirl," Edward teased.

"You changed your look but not your attitude." She poked one of his broad shoulders. "What are you doing here? Is everything alright?"

He smiled, revealing his white teeth. "It's amazing there, in the west. So I came to take you with me."

Elisa blinked. "Okay. You're probably tired after a long journey. What about having some rest and discussing it over a nice dinner?"

"That sounds good," Edward agreed. "But it's not a discussion. It's a King's order."

She took a step back. "What the hell does he want from me?"

Edward lowered his voice. "You're the only guardian who has a gifted dragon. And I bet that no one else here knows about it."

"How do *you* know?" She narrowed her eyes, her hands on her hips. Like a protective mother, she was ready to face any King and send him to hell, rather than put Jackie in danger.

He gave her a sad look. "I arrived here before Jackie, your Jackie, passed away. I was here when the dragon hatched. And with my engineering Gift, I could see –"

"Alright, I got it!" She gave him a sharp look. "But you left without saying a word."

"I was at the funeral, but you probably don't remember."

She sighed. "It was the worst week of my fucked up life."

He neared and touched her shoulders with his warm palms. "Your life has just begun, Elisa. It's a chance for you to start from a clean slate. For you and Jackie."

She started shivering against her will. Elisa had never thought she would be so vulnerable in front of any man, but Edward could see all her emotions anyway. There was no reason to hide. "I can't do it to her, Ed... She isn't ready to face this terrible, cruel reality."

"Then I'll make sure that she is ready." His voice was calm and steady. "I'm here to start your training and prepare both of you."

"For what?"

"For finding the Incapables camps and stopping the war."

She widened her eyes. "What do you mean?"

He lowered his hands. "They aren't as easy or foolish as you might have thought. They have been developing technologies and preparing something significant."

"A rebellion?" Elisa asked. She had suspected it since the day she met Eric in person. The guardians had never found him, even after checking the village. They assumed he was hiding in other Kingdoms.

"We recently arrested their gang in Esplendor," Edward confirmed her suspicions. "They are just pawns in his game, but we discovered who their leader is."

Elisa clenched her fists. "Eric."

Edward nodded. "We need you to find them. You and Jackie. Will you do it for all of us?"

"I have only one question." Elisa gave him her most confident look. "When do we start?"

To be continued...

Thank you, dear reader!

Thank you so much for reading the final story about Elisa and Jackie! Their ending is heartbreaking, but everything was meant to happen this way. Even knowing what was coming, as an author, I truly appreciate the chance to share the story about these two incredible women.

As you already know from the plot, something big is coming in this fantasy world – Incapables are growing bolder and about to start a rebellion movement. The next trilogy, *Rebellion*, is set 12 years after the events of *Forbidden Manuscript*. This time, Elisa and Lana (Yes, both of them) will unite forces to stop the war and bring the change much needed in this world. This change will help avoid future tragedies like the one that ended this book.

I'll be sharing sneak peeks into the first chapters of the next series. You can find them on my website or social media channels.

By the way, if you liked this book, you are welcome to give it a good rating! To do that, just check the store where you bought it or the *Goodreads* website. Your support means the world to me!

Sincerely yours,
-Lubov Leonova

Lubov Leonova

I always loved reading. I guess all the books I've ever read impacted me greatly - they let me expand my worldview and inspired me to pursue my dreams despite the obstacles.

Born in Russia, I immigrated to Canada in 2014, where I faced multiple challenges, including building my own life from scratch and figuring out what career path would let me use my full potential. My searches led me to feministic studies in college and volunteering in female support groups.

My experience slowly formed into ideas for my fantasy series *TwoWorlds*, where females shape the sphere of justice using their natural talents.

Today, I live on the East Coast of Canada with my husband, Alex, and our three pets: a cat, Grayson, and two sneaky bunnies – Boris and Flora.